YOU HAVE BEEN JUDGED

YOU HAVE BEEN JUDGED

JUDGE, JURY, & EXECUTIONER BOOK ONE

CRAIG MARTELLE

MICHAEL ANDERLE

You Have Been Judged (this book) is a work of fiction.

All of the characters, organizations, and events portrayed in this novel are either products of the author's imagination or are used fictitiously. Sometimes both.

Copyright © 2018 Craig Martelle and Michael Anderle
Cover copyright © LMBPN Publishing

LMBPN Publishing supports the right to free expression and the value of copyright. The purpose of copyright is to encourage writers and artists to produce the creative works that enrich our culture.

The distribution of this book without permission is a theft of the author's intellectual property. If you would like permission to use material from the book (other than for review purposes), please contact support@lmbpn.com. Thank you for your support of the author's rights.

LMBPN Publishing
PMB 196, 2540 South Maryland Pkwy
Las Vegas, NV 89109

First US edition, June 2018

The Kurtherian Gambit (and what happens within / characters / situations / worlds) are copyright © 2015-2018 by Michael T. Anderle and LMBPN Publishing.

YOU HAVE BEEN JUDGED TEAM

Thanks to our Beta Readers

Maria Stanley, Leo Roars, Sherry Foster
Micky Cocker, James Caplan, Kelly O'Donnell

Thanks to the JIT Readers

Kim Boyer
James Caplan
John Ashmore
Daniel Weigert
Peter Manis
Kelly Bowerman
Erika Everest
Kelly O'Donnell
Paul Westman
Larry Omans
Micky Cocker

If I've missed anyone, please let me know!

Editor
Lynne Stiegler

We can't write without those who support us
On the home front, we thank you for being there for us

We wouldn't be able to do this for a living if it weren't for our readers
We thank you for reading our books

INTRODUCTION

In the Etheric Federation, the terms "Barrister" and "Lawyer" are synonymous.

Judges preside over trials.

Magistrates are barristers/lawyers who also judge and mete out punishment. They are Judge, Jury and Executioner.

CHAPTER ZERO – MEET RIVKA ANOA

**O*nyx Station*
 "I hear that an All Guns Blazing franchise has just opened on Onyx Station," Charumati said.

"Your appointment with Rivka is in ten minutes, so you had best be on your way." Nathan Lowell, President of the Bad Company, stood to shake their hands.

"How much money did you lose?" Terry Henry Walton asked. He sat up straight and listened intently.

"More than I'm willing to admit. You have defeated me. I thought you were completely incapable of controlling yourself. You're a Marine, for fuck's sake! Fuck, fuck, fuck-ity, fuck. Can't you hear those words forming in your mind, ready to explode with color and imagination from the mouth that has issued a million orders over the years? 'Give it to them hard and dirty,' Patton said. You are this generation's Patton, TH. You know you want to fuck-bomb the unwashed shit-suckers out there."

"I'm not Patton, and for the record I'll take that in cash,

but that's not how things work in this Star Trek universe of yours. Post the credits to my account, my friend. Tips are always appreciated."

"*Tips?* Don't bet against Terry Henry Walton. That's the best one I have."

"Rivka?"

"She's recently arrived as an intern."

"An intern? You have *got* to be kidding me?" Terry replied.

"I know you wanted to say 'shitting me,' so let it out, Terry. Let the inner you blossom before us."

"No can do, Nathan," Char interjected, stepping between the two men. "His self-control in not swearing for months is what's going to pay for the franchise. I don't want to lose that now, so we'll be off. But an intern? I hope she knows what she's doing."

"She's more than meets the eye. I call her 'The Queen's Barrister,' if that means anything."

A young woman wearing a fashionable spacesuit approached. Terry wasn't sure whether it was armored. He resigned himself to the fact that she was new, like her spacesuit. She approached, offering her hand.

"My name is Rivka Anoa, and I'll be working with you on your franchise contract for All Guns Blazing. Do you have any questions before we start?"

"We'd like to see the All Guns Blazing before anything else. Are you old enough to go in there? You look pretty young," Terry told her.

"So do you," Rivka deftly replied. She was shorter than Char by half a head, with blonde hair, hazel eyes, and pale skin. "I'm twenty-five, I'll have you know."

"I'm *not* twenty-five, and I'd like to see what I'm going to spend Nathan's money on," Char said.

"What are you, thirty-five? That's not that big a difference."

"I think I'll be..." Terry stopped and started counting, ticking off his fingers as he went. "Round it up to one ninety. You know what that means! Somebody is going to hit the big two-oh-oh this year."

"Why?" Char rolled her eyes and groaned. "Why did you have to bring that up?"

"Because I need to throw you a surprise party," Terry replied nonchalantly.

Char turned to Rivka. "Which way to the bar? I could use a drink."

"Follow me, please." She winked at Char before shielding her mouth from Terry Henry. "I can get a wheelchair for the old guy if you'd like. I know you're not a year over twenty-nine. You look magnificent! I love your eyes."

Char loved the infectious exuberance of youth. "Lead on, Queen's Barrister. Wherever you go, we shall follow—as long as you're going to All Guns Blazing. If you're not, we'll find our own way."

They took an elevator to the promenade level, where Rivka held the doors for them to exit.

"This looks the same," Char said.

"All Guns Blazing is a brand new addition to Onyx Station. One of the signature elements is the seven by twenty-meter window looking into space. It is made using proprietary technology that will be part of the contract. The beer vats and brewing system must be purchased through The Bad Company. There is no proprietary technology there—it's just beer—but the style of vats is unique and trademarked by AGB Enterprises."

"Stop right there, barrister." Terry crossed his arms, puffed up his chest, and pushed out his biceps. "It's *never* just beer. There's an AGB Enterprises?"

"Of course. That's who owns the franchise rights, who you'll have the honor of paying a straight twenty percent of your revenue—not profit—and who you'll also have the pleasure of buying your stock materials from. It's all in the contract."

Terry deflated. "Is there any room for negotiation?"

"None, but I will remain your representative for as long as the contract remains in force."

"What if you kill somebody and can't be a lawyer anymore?"

"That is a most bizarre question. Although barristers often mete out Justice under the Yollin Accord, we don't kill people. Should I be unable to continue my duties for whatever reason, you will be provided comparable counsel from the firm. It's in the contract."

"We mete out some Justice, too," Terry started, "but I expect it's a little different from what you do."

"I've heard about what you do. I'm not sure I'd be bragging about it."

"So what do *you* think we do?"

"Assassins. You come in the dark of night and remove people perceived to be a threat to the Federation's power.

I'll tell you what, buddy, my door is locked and I can defend myself!" She pointed a finger at the two.

Terry and Char stepped back and looked at each other in confusion. "That's not what we do. We've had exactly three missions so far. We ended a civil war on Poddern, we broke a blockade at Alchon Prime, and we closed an interdimensional rift and eliminated the Skrima, a race of demon-like aliens who had come through it."

"Oh, okay!" she replied happily.

"Aren't lawyers supposed to take their clients without judging them? But more importantly, aren't lawyers supposed to research stuff? You know, get to the truth?"

"I am still new at this, but there are rumors about you and your Direct Action Branch. They're not pretty."

"What the hell?" Terry turned to Char. She shrugged. "Is Nathan fu... messing with us?"

"I hope not," Char declared, and her expression softened. "You look like you could use a beer."

Terry's ears perked up. "Could I ever! A nice dark one. Cold. Big. And then another one that looks just like it."

"I think you're going to like All Guns Blazing. It's the most popular place on Onyx Station." They turned a corner and Rivka waved her hands as if making the bar magically appear.

There was a fight going on at the entrance. Rivka held her hand up, signaling for them to stop.

"Wait a minute," Char said. She and Terry pushed past the barrister and ran for the entrance. Half the Bad Company warriors who had arrived with Terry and Char were inside the bar playing a drinking game, and the other half were already drunk and trying to get in. The bouncers were having none of it.

"We've been here thirty minutes! How can they be drunk already? How can they be in a fight? How does crap like this happen?"

Terry grabbed the closest warrior and hauled him backward. The man tried to throw a haymaker as he swung around, but TH dodged it and slammed the man on his face. Char rabbit-punched the next man. Terry kicked the third in the back of the knee. When the man started to stumble, Terry punched him on the top of his head.

The fight ended quickly after that. The bouncers were unscathed and stood with their arms crossed, watching Terry and Char with wary eyes.

"Form up, you knotheads," Terry growled at them. Six men and three women, all drunk and bruised, responded with alacrity. "You lasted a grand total of thirty minutes. That's not a record, so, while you're confined to the *War Axe*, be comfortable in the knowledge that there are people in this universe who are stupider than you. How in the hell did you get drunk in thirty minutes?"

"A killer drink in one of the sub-level bars. The Supernova Hellspawn something or other," one of them mumbled.

"Get back to the *War Axe*. I will have Smedley track you, and if any of you geniuses get lost, you won't be confined to the ship. You'll be in the brig, don't pass go, don't collect two hundred dollars, and don't ever enjoy one minute of liberty for the rest of your natural-born days."

The group looked contrite until one of the women started puking. She remained at attention throughout the affair, leaving a splatter on the deck before her and a trail down the front of her shirt. The others started to giggle.

"You had best get back to the ship. Right. Now." Terry waved at them angrily. They started to run, but they had turned in different directions. Two fell, but all avoided the spew. They helped each other up, decided on the way to go, and dashed away.

"Isn't the hangar deck the other way?" Char asked.

"Yup."

Rivka stood to the side, covering her nose with her hand to avoid the smell. Terry grinned at her. "Not our finest moment, counselor. If you wondered about any night-sneaking by steely-eyed ghosts, what you saw here today should put those rumors to rest. And you're probably thinking we can't fight our way out of a wet paper bag. To the untrained eye it may seem that way, but these people have been in combat for a long time. They're blowing off steam, that's all."

Continuing to cover her nose while turning so she didn't have to look at the mess, Rivka asked, "Maybe you can teach me a move or two? That was pretty good, how you disarmed three of them in three seconds."

"They weren't armed," Terry countered.

"You know what I mean," she huffed. She nodded to the bouncers, who waved them in. "After you."

Terry opted for seats at the bar, with his back to the window. He would look at space later. He needed to observe the bar and understand the potential.

Rivka waited patiently as he inspected everything in sight, methodically looking from one feature to the next.

"He's memorizing all of it."

"I'll transmit a complete portfolio of pictures. They come with the franchise license."

"Sure, but he already has the whole bar committed to his eidetic memory. After one hundred and ninety years you'd think his brain would be full, but it's not. Maybe when he gets to be my age..."

"I heard that," Terry interjected. "Nothing you can say will get a rise out of me, not while I'm here in this beautiful thing."

The bartender handed over a perfectly-pulled pint, so dark that no light passed through the glass. Terry looked at it as if he were in love. He closed his eyes as he sipped it, keeping the glass close as he licked his lips and took another long, slow drink.

"I may never swear again," Terry suggested after he had finished the beer and called for a second.

"Bullshit!" Char declared. "Once the bar is up and running, you'll be your old self. If you're going to drink the profits, I'll cut you off!"

"What?"

"Our bar. It's our *bar*, not Terry Henry Walton's private watering hole."

"Ooh." Rivka pursed her lips and brought up the contract on her pad. "I'll need to make some changes."

"Charumati Walton, co-owner. Equally, if you please," Char specified. Terry took a big gulp and coughed before smiling.

"It's every man's dream. I get to own a bar with my woman!" Terry declared loudly.

"For fuck's sake! What kind of barbarian is this turning

you into?" Char leaned back on her barstool to glare at Terry.

"*There's* the woman I love. Co-owners of a wildly-successful business enterprise, bringing entertainment, food, and drink to those who want to enjoy themselves for a brief period of time.

"You two are weird," Rivka remarked without looking up.

Char stood and motioned for Terry to finish his beer, which he dutifully accomplished with little fanfare. "We're going shopping. Buzz us when you have the documents ready. I think All Guns Blazing is exactly what we need. And a new pair of shoes. Maybe an outfit to go with them. A purse, too. I almost never carry one, but who knows? Especially if it's a good match for the outfit."

"By all that's holy in this bald monkey-ass world, don't make me sign any more papers!"

"I assure you that no one is making you do anything. That premise alone could void this packet of contracts. Are you making that accusation?"

"No," Terry admitted sheepishly. "I meant to ask if we will we ever be fucking done signing our fucking lives away?"

"You are an angry man," Rivka told him. She climbed down from the barstool and stood to her full height, and she was still shorter than a sitting TH. "I have a job to do, and I don't think you respect it! Nathan asked me to do this as a personal favor. Yes. I'm an intern. Yes. I'm a woman. Get over that and do your job, and I'll do mine!"

"He doesn't have anything against you being an intern or a woman," Char clarified, pointing at the sheaf of papers. "He despises bureaucrats who embrace paperwork as the epitome of productivity."

"You think I like this?"

"How could you not?" Terry declared.

"Okay, maybe I do, but it's in the sense of putting a puzzle together so that there are no holes. You will be able to defend your bar before the Queen and the universe! No one can take it away from you, except for AGB Enterprises if you violate the branding or fail to make your purchases from them or fail to pay them, although you've made that payment automatic by agreeing to use AGB Enterprises' Accounting and Banking system as declared on this form." Rivka dug halfway through the stack and pointed to a page.

Terry didn't bother to look at the document. He was amazed by the victorious look on her face.

"I feel like there should be a fist-pump or something."

Her smile evaporated, and she repeated, "You are an angry man."

A drunk patron pounded on the bar, demanding service. The bartender waved him off, refusing to serve him. The drunk man slid close to Rivka.

"Whatcha got there?" he asked as he pushed Rivka and reached a dirty hand toward the pile of papers. Rivka caught him by the wrist.

"Don't touch the contract," she told him, her voice low and steady.

"Don't touch me!" he replied and grabbed for her. She

let go, caught an ear in each hand, and pulled his head downward. She drove her leg upward. His face met her knee, and that was the end of the confrontation.

"Assault, battery, and interference in a confidential attorney-client conversation." He moaned and held his face. She kicked him in the ribs. "Justice is served."

"Holy crap!" Terry looked at her with newfound respect. "You can do that? Judge, jury, and executioner?"

She looked at the man rolling around on the floor. "No one was executed, but yes I can. We are authorized to mete out Justice when the cases are clear-cut, like this one. There's video. He's guilty, so fuck that guy."

"If someone messes with our bar, are you going to fuck *them* up, too?" Terry asked with a big smile.

"Not if you don't sign those contracts," she countered.

TH turned to Char. "I love my lawyer."

"Of course, you do, now keep signing."

Terry Henry's contract was the last legal matter she completed as an intern. In the eyes of the Queen, she had never been just an intern. Rivka Anoa had always been the Queen's Barrister, a gifted champion for Justice...

1

The Judge flowed through the door to loom over the court. The trial had come to a close, and it was the moment of truth, or maybe the moment of Justice. Barrister Anoa had built a sound case and argued well.

The jury would have to put him away. She nodded politely to the defense. Atticus "Custer" Tikabow, her old friend, had been her opponent, although the lawyers themselves didn't look at things that way. They argued different points of law. The jury decided, and the counsels wiped their hands of it all and went back to their offices. Or the golf course. The Judges had to mete out punishment. In cases without a jury, they heard the evidence, ruled, and ordered the punishment carried out instantly.

Punishment up to and including death. Custer's client was slimy and came across as a weasel. He sat closest to the jury, so they had to see it. His mere presence had been enough for them to decide. Her brilliant arguments had been frosting on the cake.

She remained standing, confident and proud.

"Would the jury read the verdict?" the Judge ordered. The courtroom remained standing while the Judge leaned back in his recliner.

"The jury finds the defendant not guilty."

"What?" Rivka blurted as her eyes shot to the defendant.

Custer and the man were hugging. He winked at her over his counsel's shoulder. She was furious, and her head started to swim. She leaned on the table to keep from falling over.

"My appreciation goes to the jury for your work in this case. You are released from your duties." The Judge intoned the words as he did at the end of every jury trial. "Defendant is free to go."

A phrase rarely heard, since the evidence was usually clear by the time it went to court. People pled to lesser crimes to avoid the harshness of a trial sentence.

The Judge stood and walked out.

Rivka looked frantically around the courtroom. A din of voices filled the air and visitors were filing out the back. The jury was leaving by a side door. The defendant and Custer were arm in arm, chatting like old friends.

"But he did it!" she blurted.

"Nope," Custer replied. Her colleague was easy on the eyes. He'd won, and she'd lost. She shook his hand as decorum dictated, but she wanted to crush it.

And him.

The defendant leaned past his lawyer to grab Rivka by the arm and yanked her toward him. Emotions and images flooded her mind. Overwhelming joy at being set free.

Disdain for the system that couldn't find him guilty, when *he had done it*! She saw the murder clearly in his mind, and she *knew* he was just getting started.

He had hissed something at her, but she didn't hear it since the images were so overwhelming. The Queen had known of her gift, but Rivka generally kept her hands to herself. She considered it an invasion of others' privacy to see their random thoughts—but sometimes the thoughts weren't so random.

"Murderer!" she snarled. The defendant started to laugh and winked again before thanking his lawyer one last time and walking away.

Custer looked at her, but her expression told him to hold his tongue. He nodded curtly and followed his client out.

What the hell just happened? Rivka wondered. *A fucking murderer walks free?* "No!"

The courtroom's paneled walls absorbed the sound of her anguish. *Sometimes the law doesn't always do what we want. Better that nine guilty men walk free than one innocent man goes to jail.*

She recalled that from her law-school lectures, as well as the old adage, "You can't win 'em all."

It didn't make her feel any better.

"I deserve a drink!" she declared to the empty court. "If it would please Your Honor, I'm outta here. Maybe through the dull pounding of a hangover, I can figure out what the fuck went wrong. If nothing else, tonight I'm going to drown that shit."

Rivka blinked the fog away. A bloody knife was in her hand, and she looked at it stupidly. "Where'd you come from?" she asked the blade. It didn't answer.

The blood was fresh; still crimson, not yet starting to darken. She shook the knife, and a couple of drops flew off.

"Damn!" she exclaimed when one hit her pants. She shook her leg, but there it was —a stain she'd have to wash out. When she put her foot down, she saw the body. She'd almost stepped on it. "Where'd *you* come from?"

She crouched near it and checked his neck for a pulse with her left hand. Still warm. No rigor mortis.

And no pulse. She looked at the knife still clutched in her hand. She tossed it away and looked closer at the victim. "Oh no," she moaned when she saw who it was. "You deserve to die for what you did, but not here. Not like this."

Her boots were in the growing puddle of blood, and her fingers were stained. Her prints were on the knife. "Oh no," she moaned again, ramming her eyes shut as she forced her mind to tell her what happened.

Booze. Rage. *The murderer!*

She saw herself follow him. He'd led her into an alley where he'd confronted her; asked her if she knew what it was like to make love to a winner. The rage had taken over. The knife was his. He had tried to defend himself with it.

And failed.

Her mind raced. *Actus reus*, the act of committing the crime, had been completed. *Mens rea*, her mental state, was irrelevant. Prima facie, "on the face of it," as the Latin would describe, she was guilty as sin.

"Fuck this," she told the corpse. "See you in court, bitch."

She stood and started to walk away, but her knees were weak. She wasn't like him, okay with killing in cold blood. He had pulled the knife, but she had already attacked him. Would she lie to protect herself? No—but she wouldn't incriminate herself either. When the authorities came, she'd stay silent. The burden of proof was on them.

It wouldn't take much.

"You fucker," she growled. "Not happy with taking one life, you have to take two." She wanted to spit on him, but didn't want to leave her DNA. She picked up the knife and wiped off the handle, then dropped it back on the ground.

She sneered as she walked past the corpse.

I could use a cup of coffee, she thought with false bravado. Her head started to swim. Guilt. Pain. His emotional cry of victory still ringing in her mind. She staggered as if drunk, although since the effects of the booze had already dissipated, she shouldn't have been. She raged against it, stopping to collect herself.

"A cup of coffee will be good," she said aloud as if trying to convince herself. With a calmer spirit she walked from the alley, stopping when a police unit pulled up. An officer jumped out and fixed her with a stare. "Can I help you?" she asked.

"Yes, by getting on your knees and putting your hands on top of your head."

"Well, that's not how I expected this night to end," she remarked weakly.

Rivka knew where she was the instant she awoke. She didn't remember them stunning her, or the chase which had quite likely preceded it, but she did know where she was.

A Federation holding cell, gray and cramped and silent. She had seen them often enough, but never from the inside.

It was a tiny windowless thing, and the metal of the walls was unadorned save for a small digital screen to her left, momentarily blank. It was protected by a shield of shatter-proof glass.

Below it was a single line of script: Etheric Federation Intergalactic. She frowned.

She was in a holding cell in the intergalactic quarter, which meant they were taking her into space—which was well outside the norm for an open-and-shut case. She tried to think through the implications, but the cell felt like it was closing in. She needed her office. Her datapad. Access to the legal database. She needed freedom and information, neither of which were available.

She was left with speculation, which was the worst way to think.

Rivka saw two possibilities.

One, they were sending her to Jhiordaan, the penal planet of the Federation, and––if the stories were true––a living nightmare.

That option seemed unlikely. Her killing of the man had not only been unjustified, it would leave a deep scar on the reputation of the Federation. Lawyers weren't supposed to kill defendants who had been found not guilty.

Not ever. Although not guilty was a far cry from innocent.

Two, public execution. She had thought they would be as eager as possible to punish her, to dispel any doubt as to their integrity.

Option two seemed most likely, yet she was in an intergalactic holding cell. She needed more information.

The door to her cell hissed open and she greeted the sound like a breath of fresh air. She stood with her hands behind her back, ready to interrogate whoever entered to get the information she needed to better understand her situation and better plan her future.

"What the hell?"

Custer.

"You!" She spat the word with all the hatred she could summon, lips twisting in a vicious snarl. "That man was guilty, damn you! How *dare* you come here? You, who defended a murderer and let him--"

"I came to say goodbye." His voice was barely above a whisper, yet it sliced somehow through the fury of her words. "You're going to see the High Chancellor, Rivka. I don't know why, but I know that much. It could be good for you. I figured you'd like to know."

How she hated him for this compassion when *he* should be the one to hang.

He sighed and shook his head. "Perhaps they will let you live. I cannot say, but we can hope--"

"I don't *want* your hope!" she yelled. A volcano of inner rage threatened to erupt. "You defended a murderer, Custer! You helped him beat the system!"

"I was doing my job, just like you," he countered. Anger

flashed across his face before his expression softened. "I thought it was a losing case, too. I don't know what happened."

"One day the truth will come out!" she yelled. "One day they'll know. They'll see what you defended! One *damned* day, the world--"

He shook his head and turned away, slamming the door in her face.

I need information and what do I do? All the talking. I'm a dumbass. I could have asked why I'm in an Intergalactic cell. Who is hearing the case? What does the public know? So many questions and I squander them on a self-righteous "fuck you." So, I've got that going for me, she thought.

The High Chancellor? What could he possibly want? But only silence answered her. She did a set of pushups, then sit-ups, then more pushups. *Don't want to be all flabby when I say goodbye in the sparky chair.*

2

Why would Custer stop by? It wasn't to taunt her. They'd been friends, of a sort. Maybe colleague was a better term, but they had been that before becoming two people who could enjoy each other's company over a beer.

That was before he had defended a murderer. Could she separate the person from the act? Maybe someday, but not today. As a lawyer, he was well-versed in massaging the truth. Some would say "lie," but not Rivka. She knew how to see through that. She had been trained for it, but she was gifted in it, too.

"I love the law," she told her cell. And it was that very same law that was going to condemn her. She embraced the title of Barrister. It made her sound stately.

And old. She liked the impression that left with people. The Queen's Barrister. People expected an old guy, but then she showed up—short, smiling, and young.

Too young to be executed.

The cell door hissed open. She waited with her hands behind her, thinking calm thoughts to help her keep from biting the next person's head off. She hoped it was Custer. Not to apologize. Never that. But to ask the questions she wanted answers to.

This time it was the guards she had expected last time, the ones who would take her to her fate. To her legally-delivered Justice.

A hulking Federation guard leaned in, ready with a stun club. She tilted her head. The man was twice her size. She couldn't try to run past him since he filled the doorway.

"Really?" Rivka blurted before holding her hands in front of her so she could be cuffed.

"Really?" he parroted as he flexed the muscles of one arm. He stepped aside and pointed to the doorway. She let her hands fall to her sides.

"Am I supposed to run so you can shoot me while trying to escape?" she asked, backing deeper into the cell.

"And I thought I hated fucking lawyers on the outside. The High Chancellor wants to see your dumb ass."

"You know what they say," she started. He looked at her blankly. "Everybody likes a little ass, but nobody likes a smartass. I'm not sure about a dumbass, though."

The man shook his head as he chuckled. He jabbed a thumb toward the door after adopting an angry scowl.

"What does the High Chancellor want with me?" she asked.

The guard rolled his eyes, shook his head, and herded her toward the door. Three guards waited outside, each more massive than the one before. Resigned to her fate, she shuffled into the corridor and assumed her position in the middle of the man-box. Together they stepped off, the guards looking straight ahead.

She studied them as if their demeanor would suggest what was coming. None of them gave anything away. Her mind was free from intruding thoughts. She brushed against one of the guards, hoping contact would help her see what he was thinking. He pushed her away from him, but not before she saw the image of someone in his mind. She checked his ring finger and saw the gold band. He was thinking of his wife.

"Are you allowed to speak?" she persisted, wishing she were taller.

"There's nothing for us to talk about. Nothing that matters, anyway." The man who flanked her on the right sounded as if his mouth were full of gravel.

Well, that's cheerful. Rivka stopped trying. "I have plenty to talk about and lots of questions. Maybe you can answer some for me: why am I being held in the intergalactic section?"

She had not worked on this side--the disciplinary side--of Justice; she had only helped determine who was guilty. She left sentencing to the Judges. Sometimes that meant capital crimes; crimes for which a person could be executed.

She had never wondered what it was like for the men who executed prisoners; who saw the sentences carried out. The guards were only tools of Justice, just as she was. Knives to carve the cancers, as the legal system determined them to be, out of society. Cancers, as she told juries they were.

She'd never imagined she might be the one cut by the very blade she had touted as sacrosanct.

It was a short walk to the High Chancellor's office, but her mind raced through a broad range of possibilities. None of them made any sense. All were bald-faced speculation, the type barristers despised because it served no purpose. Distill the evidence and present it to the jury, who determined what fact was and wasn't. That was how it worked.

"What kind of music do you listen to?" she asked to fill the void.

"How about you shut the fuck up and hear the sound of silence?"

"That's a good one. How about we add a big bucket of blow me to the playlist?" Rivka wasn't good at taking a miscarriage of Justice lying down. If she was going to be sent to Jhiordaan or executed, she had nothing to lose. "We could play *Hall of the Mountain King*."

"I do like that one," one of the other guards agreed as he stepped aside to show her into the High Chancellor's chambers.

Rumor had it that High Chancellor Wyatt was a vampire. Rivka didn't know. She had seen no evidence one way or another. In person, he seemed human. Some said that he did not drink blood. Others said he feasted on prisoners before they were executed, and that was why the execution count was so high in his jurisdiction. They were the High Chancellor's buffet. Rivka doubted it.

Bullshit, she thought. *He looks like a normal guy.*

Seated in his ornate mahogany chair and dressed in the somber black robes of his office, he looked casually over the top of a datapad he'd been reading. His eyes seemed to glow red as he looked at Rivka and she froze in place. It was terrifying, but in a bizarrely civil way. Perhaps it was the Judge's accoutrements that softened the blow.

The High Chancellor was supposedly an ancient creature, steeped in years of courtroom battle. Backroom whispers claimed he had been hand-picked by the former Empress Bethany Anne herself for biological enhancement, his body programmed with nanocytes that gave him many of the same physical and mental capabilities vampires of old had enjoyed.

Even among lawyers there was little known about him —other than the fact that he was stern and merciless and commanded a flawless knowledge of Federation law. He had been promoted from his position as a human prosecutor on Yoll after an impressive series of courtroom victories. After rising to High Chancellor, he had reportedly enjoyed complete success in enforcing Federation Justice throughout the empire.

Vampires, it turned out, received less resistance than humans.

"Rivka Anoa. You have killed a man." His cheekbones, ears, and slanted eyes were illuminated by a pair of yellow-shaded lamps flanking his massive desk. "You are a lawyer of the Federation, and you killed a man judged not guilty?"

His eyebrows were high, pencil-thin, and arched in silent accusation.

Rivka had planned on remaining silent, but this wasn't the court. He didn't need her testimony to judge her and execute her on the spot. The guards had gone. Her hands were free. The High Chancellor pointed to a chair, but she remained standing.

"Yes," Rivka replied. "Yes, High Chancellor. I...I killed him. He was cleared, free to go. And then I killed him."

How could this possibly go well? What in all hells had Custer been raving about, with all that talk of sparing me? "I'm a damned lawyer—a barrister—and I killed an innocent man. Or one *judged* innocent, at least, although he most assuredly was not..."

Rivka's diatribe trailed off, jaw tightening as she realized how absurd she sounded. She didn't have the slightest chance. "He was guilty, High Chancellor!" she blurted desperately. So much for protocol. "He was guilty, and I felt it. I knew it, though I can't explain why."

The High Chancellor frowned, a grave but mild twisting of the lips which morphed gradually to a deeper scowl. He shifted in his chair, and one slender-fingered hand rose above the surface of his desk. In it he clutched a graceful jeweled dagger, double-edged, which he twirled lightly. He seemed not to notice in the slightest, but Rivka found herself transfixed, staring at the weapon. Did he mean to frighten her?

I'm about to die, she lamented bitterly. *Am I not frightened enough already?*

"You knew he was guilty, but you cannot explain why. Unfortunate. If you killed a man without explanation, how can Justice save you? If you killed a man with legal justification, however..." He shrugged with theatrical vagueness.

What? Rivka stared at him in mounting bewilderment. Justice wasn't supposed to save her, not *her* specifically. It was supposed to save society; ensure that rightness prevailed. "If I killed a man *without* legal justification, High Chancellor?"

"Laws can be adjusted. Hearts, some say, cannot." He grinned. She wasn't sure if she had seen vampire's fangs. "If you killed a man and had any sort of explanation, lawful or unlawful, then I would hear it, Barrister." The dagger spun in his ancient fingers, blade glinting yellow in the gentle lamplight.

"It was like I…" She stumbled for a moment, grasping for words which would not make her sound insane. "Like I fell into his mind and brushed against his thoughts. I couldn't hear them, not really, but I could feel them…" She shook her head helplessly.

"I don't know what it was like!" she conceded before boldly meeting his crimson eyes. "I felt his emotions, his joy at having gotten away with murder, his arrogance that he was above the law, and I knew that he was guilty. I also knew he would do it again, so if he walked away, more innocents would lose their lives."

She waited for a chain of straining heartbeats, confident in her conviction but afraid it would not sway him. He seemed to be staring into and through her, and yet at the same time had forgotten she was there. The knife spun between his fingers, utterly silent and never slowing.

"High Chancellor?" she began tenuously. "I felt his guilt, but…" She tried not to sound like an idiot. "I still don't know why I killed him, not really. I was shocked after the trial. I needed some time to get away, to walk, to have a drink. I have no idea what compelled me to confront him or why I decided to kill him, but I did. I remember it clearly enough. I expect I'm supposed to feel bad about it, but I don't. Does that make me a psychopath?"

The High Chancellor finally looked away. "It makes you something," he said vaguely before leaning forward to fix her with his piercing gaze again. "You hear things in your mind, you say? Feelings and thoughts?"

"No. I mean, yes, High Chancellor. It hasn't happened before, at least not as intensely as this. And not proper thoughts, in the sense of words and sentences. More like random emotions and images." She struggled to find the words. "I can feel each distinct individual and sense their emotions, but it all blurs together. It's such a storm I can hardly tell one person from the next, let alone pick out what they are actually thinking. It's more of just a--"

He interrupted her by coughing once and raising a hand for silence. With ease he stopped spinning the dagger, although he still grasped it by its glittering hilt. In the space of a breath, it vanished somewhere into his robes.

She couldn't feel anything from the High Chancellor; no emotion, no random thoughts. It was as if she were standing by herself in an empty room.

The High Chancellor stood and rolled back his billowy sleeves with businesslike resolve, snatching a quill and paper from his desk. Rivka stifled a flutter of surprise, realizing he had been slouching the entire time, his figure hidden by his robes. And those forearms! She had thought him as an old creature, still sharp of mind but fading beyond his physical prime. All worn and ragged corners and angles, like a desk with years of varnish rubbed away.

But beneath the thickness of his robes, High Chancellor Wyatt was huge, a looming specimen of a man with a trim waist and a chest as broad as twice her shoulders. Even performing such a simple task as lifting the pen his forearms rippled with muscle, traced by a network of veins so prominent she was surprised they did not burst from his skin.

Rivka wondered distantly what he did in his free time to maintain such a body which so perfectly reflected physical power.

"Rivka Anoa," he began mildly, the words incongruously gentle for a vampire. The rumors... But then again, what if the rumors weren't true? "Are you aware that the Queen's Rangers have been disbanded?"

What? "I am," she stated simply. *What does that have to do with anything?*

"Yes, indeed." The High Chancellor nodded. "The Queen's Rangers were deemed a hazard and a liability to Federation integrity. They were too obvious a violation of the universal accountability we hope to maintain over our constituency. There were numerous complaints. Talk of convictions made without the law, of action without oversight and nonexistent consequences. The title 'Rangers,' it seems, spoke far too much of vigilantes in the night."

Rivka nodded, and her mind raced in a new direction.

As the man said, the Queen's Rangers had acted completely without oversight and left in their wake both chaos and peace, a storm of bureaucratic destruction which had been torturous for Rivka's branch to remedy. She had always entertained the private fancy that if she ever met a Ranger, she'd punch him squarely in the face and then ask him if that helped him see the need for lawyers.

High Chancellor Wyatt smiled at her confusion, fangs bright white against the ruby hardness of his lips. "Complaints, yes. Some claimed they enacted violence without the clarity of law.'"

Just as they had done, so had she. "And the Rangers were punished accordingly, High Chancellor?" Of course. She should have seen it coming.

"No." He smiled unnervingly. "The Rangers themselves claimed they enacted 'Justice without the twisting of the law,' so we changed their names. We formally disbanded them, retrained them, and reassigned those people. They are now called 'Magistrates.'"

Rivka blinked. "You took Rangers and made them lawyers?" She had always thought of Rangers as a horde of trigger-happy cowboys set loose upon the universe.

"Meting out Justice is not for the faint of heart."

The High Chancellor studied her intently, and she grunted uncertainly. "I guess I never..." she started to say, but stopped when he shook his head.

"I have business to attend to!" He smiled brightly. "You have given me much to think about. Guards!"

The door opened and the guards filed in, surrounded her, and led her away.

She replayed the conversation in her head start to finish, and then again. By the time they showed her into a cell, she realized that she was in a different place. She had been so absorbed, she didn't remember which way they'd come.

"Dammit!" she exclaimed.

"There she is," the first guard said, giving her a hearty push and closing the door behind her. It whooshed shut with a certain finality. Gone were days of a large deadbolt slammed into the frame with the forlorn click of a heavy lock.

"Fine!" she yelled after them, shaking her head at her failure to gather information. She chided herself, "You might be a good barrister, but you suck as an investigator."

She made a face and stuck out her tongue at the closed door.

"You suck, too," she told no one in particular.

She sat on the floor of the barren cell and began to explore her mind, looking for hidden answers to her questions. The High Chancellor's words played over and over. He had told her everything and nothing at the same time.

The epitome of a barrister's conversation.

When she finally fell asleep, it was to the constant thrum of Rangers stealing through the night wearing the robes of a Magistrate.

3

Rivka awoke with a start. "Son of a bitch," she grumbled when she realized that she was still in her cell.

The door was open and light flooded in.

"What now, butt stains?" she asked when a pair of guards entered.

"Let's go," one of them ordered, and they led her into the corridor. Silently one of the guards grasped her by the elbow, helping guide her down the corridor.

She felt no anger or subterfuge from him. She wanted that to calm her, but it didn't. The only sound was the echo of their boots on the metal floor. A forlorn noise, harbinger of a one-way trip.

She tried to maintain her dignity as they walked, even though she was unsure the last time she'd had a shower. And she had to pee.

"Potty break for the perp?" she asked. They stonewalled her and kept walking.

As her eyes slowly adjusted, Rivka realized they were leading her to the transport hangar. If they had been moving her somewhere on the planet, they would have taken her a different way.

They are sending me to space.

She glanced sideways at her guards, knowing they wouldn't tell her. Rumors of the penal planet Jhiordaan leapt into her mind. Speculation, the destroyer of all reason. "Fuck off," she mumbled.

Rivka also cursed within her mind, wishing she could have a few more moments with the High Chancellor. Just a few more…but it wasn't to be. Lamenting the past was as useful as speculation. Like her impending trip to Jhiordaan.

Not going to Jhiordaan, dumbass! she tried to tell herself. *What's your game, High Chancellor? Some of us don't play as well as you.*

Some of us aren't even in the same stadium. Or the city where the stadium is located, she corrected.

Her guards were distinctly grim and silent—even more so than the last, if that were possible. *Jhiordaan for sure,* she thought with dread, studying their stony gazes. *No execution for me, but I have been condemned to something worse than death as an act of mercy for the mad.*

But men did not become this hard from taking prisoners just anywhere. Men became this hard from taking prisoners to hell over and over and over again. It no longer bothered them, as she'd thought when earlier she had touched the guard.

They were insulated from the pain. She fought to maintain a barrister's dignity—do the crime, do the time—yet her knees grew weak.

A guard grabbed her arm and half-carried her to a waiting motorized cart. He unceremoniously dumped her into a seat and slid in beside her, bumping her into the middle. The other guard climbed in the other side.

"I'm not liking this man sandwich," she remarked, looking at them. The guards refused to meet her gaze. "Can't you fuckers talk? What the hell? I'm on my way to some shithole, and you give me the stone face."

"Stop that." One of the guards shook her roughly, but she saw his eyes soften with compassion.

So they weren't completely devoid of feeling.

The transport hangar was a colossal place, with a high vaulted ceiling reinforced by enormous ribs of steel. Beneath its spreading dome were dozens of varied spacecraft arrayed in harmonious chaos. Sleek and silvery fighters lined the flanks of the room, positioned for speedy departures. Hulking freighters towered above her in the very center, three of them with loading doors swung wide and a steady stream of hovercarts ferrying cargo to and from. Scattered around was a motley collection of lesser craft—transports and interplanetary cruisers. There were even a couple deep-space Seekers.

Rivka remembered her childhood fascination with Seekers. That was the common term for the Empire's exploration ships, the ones outfitted to venture into uncharted quadrants far beyond the range of standard intergalactic travel. She had always dreamed of joining a Seeker crew one day, and perhaps even piloting the ship herself.

Her smile slipped, then broke. She didn't think they recruited Seekers from Jhiordaan.

Silently the cart wove through men bustling about with hovercarts or boxes or bundles of hoses. One company of blue-suited pilots trotted in formation across the cart's path, straps flapping loosely from the white uniform helmets in their hands.

They saluted her guards as they passed, but Rivka hardly noticed. It all became a soundless blur—colors without meaning—as she traveled closer to the next step in her incarceration.

They took her to a tiny intraorbital shuttle, nothing more than a cockpit and a single passenger's seat into which she was manacled, facing aft.

One of the guards was apparently a pilot, because he buckled himself into the cockpit in front of her and dismissed his comrade with a wave. The ship's thrusters engaged with a steady hum and the craft slid smoothly towards the vast open portal of the hangar.

Rivka wondered desperately how hard it would be to free herself. Perhaps she could feign unconsciousness, or wait until they landed and the man came back to free her. Maybe they would still be alone in the moments before he led her outside wherever they landed. Her hands would still be bound, of course, but perhaps she could lash out with a foot and kick his pistol away, leap across the gap between them and smash him in the—

Idiot! He's armed and trained to handle violent criminals. These men had her trussed, and she was as helpless as a kitten. She couldn't try anything even if she wanted to.

The pilot's body blocked her forward view, but a tiny

square window was set into the cargo door of the transport. Through it, she could make out the hangar's organized chaos as they pulled away.

The ship swept into the open sky and the city that had only recently become Rivka's home dwindled away beneath her, a massive sprawl of stately domes and gleaming spires interwoven with hordes of lesser buildings, squat and tiny, clustered close together like so many child's blocks.

Rivka stared out the side window as the ship raced upward, marveling at the chaos and insignificance of it all. It was so *small*. And then it too was gone, melding into the tangled patchwork of hues and textures that defined the surface of her world. Shining cities and barren wilderness and scraps of drifting cloud obscured from Rivka's eyes. Land stretched away in all directions, and the metal borders of her tiny window blocked the horizon from her view.

Farther still, and she could see the globe itself. They drifted away from it with a smoothness and silence and finality that made her breath catch.

She knew there were other things out there, of course. Countless things. Worlds and races and entire other *galaxies*.

Rivka had known, all her life that it was the Queen's vision to see them connected. She had heard the stories and watched the videos. She'd known, in a vague and detached way, that she was contributing to something larger; something which stretched beyond the narrow, winding streets where she pursued her work.

But to see it all rush away beneath her?

There was a sudden tiny *click*, barely perceptible, and Rivka realized that the ship had stopped moving. She waited, forcing her mind away from speculation of the next horrible thing, and then the next. Rivka collected data, the information she would use to shape her perception and make her case. That was what barristers did. It was her comfort zone.

"Let's go." The pilot stood and approached her from the cockpit, grabbing her by the arm and unshackling her from the chair. He dragged her to her feet as if she weighed no more than a whisper. "Out."

"Where are we?" she managed to ask, but he didn't answer. He led her to the hatch, and she clambered up the ladder at his direction. He followed her up, watching her warily. Her shackles weighed her down and she was unable to resist, although she wasn't sure she even wanted to. Rivka had more data to collect before she could pass judgment. Speculation was the mind-killer, and her mind was fresh and vibrant. It was her strength.

It wouldn't fail her now.

The ship quivered slightly from a force somewhere outside, and the chamber echoed with a series of metallic clicks. After a moment the hatch slid open to reveal a boarding corridor attached to the top of the shuttle.

We didn't land, she realized. *We are outside of another ship or we—*

Two pairs of muscled arms hauled her out, setting her not ungently on her feet. "Where are we?" she asked in as firm a voice as she could muster while trying to peek out around the massive bodies of her two new guards. The broad windows of the corridor revealed nothing except the void of space and a scattering of feeble stars. Her stomach lurched.

The hatch leading to the shuttle closed. Her previous guard would be returning home. Being handed over to the new guards felt like one more nail in her coffin. She sighed heavily and trundled along with her keepers, powerless to do anything besides wait and see what there was to see.

Gentle as they might have been, they did not answer. Without so much as a nod for the pilot who had brought her here the two men marched her down another long metallic corridor and through a series of chambers.

All around her people scurried or stood in earnest conversation, peering into monitors and chattering into headphones and gesturing toward an assortment of display screens on the wall. There were windows in several of the chambers, and through one she saw the tiny blue-green orb of the planet, swept by pale clouds which looked as solid as ice from such a distance.

It's so small! she marveled, and wondered at the countless millions that comprised just the known universe.

Rivka's curiosity spiked when they led her to a tiny white-walled chamber and left without a word. A long mirror lined one wall, and there was a single table in the center with two chairs, one on each side. There were no decorations on the walls. *An interrogation room?*

She had expected to be taken to a cell to wait for the transport to Jhiordaan. Speculation.

The door slid smoothly open, and a man walked in. *A soldier,* Rivka judged, taking in the toned lines of his body and the hardness of his face. His barrister's uniform was crisp and well-cut. He folded his arms in front of him.

What does the data tell you? she asked herself.

"You're not a barrister," Rivka told him evenly. "Not like the ones *I've* met, anyway. You're a Ranger."

Not a question. *Don't ask a question you don't know the answer to. Lawyer 101.*

He raised a finger to his lips. "We don't say that word anymore, Barrister. Nobody does, and one day we hope it will be forgotten." His eyes were stern, but they held an unmistakable warmth.

Hope. That spider silk-thin tendril she grasped had become a rope, maybe even a ladder, and she felt herself climbing toward a radiant light.

"I see you have a million questions. They'll get answered in due time," he interrupted calmly, motioning for her to sit. She did so, leaning forward in her seat, her attention focused like a laser on the man before her. "I'm not a fan of ultimatums, but there are two possible outcomes here. One is completely in my control. The other is outside it." He grunted and trailed off for a moment, studying her with casual indifference.

Desperately she strained to calm herself. If this were a test, she had to pass. She steeled her nerves and donned a mask of confidence.

"If you wish to keep your position as Queen's Barrister, you will join us. You will learn how to handle yourself in a fight, and how to use a variety of weapons." He chuckled ever so slightly. "You'll become the sort of person I'm guessing your type usually curses as the spawn of chaos—the seed of the universe's bureaucratic nightmares."

"'*My* type?'" She smiled before ducking her head.

"Maybe you're right. I've heard stories about *your* type, too."

He held a finger to his lips once again and lost his fight to keep his face neutral. His smile flickered and died, and he leaned forward with frightening intensity. "When you see the filth that's out there you'll understand why we need proper killers, not just anointed executioners."

She studied him as if waiting for a punchline. The words raced through her mind but blurting an answer didn't seem right, not when she hadn't heard all the options.

"Option two. You face your fate as a prisoner of the Federation, convicted of capital murder. You and I part ways. Your life becomes little more than a document in our legal system, ferried from one desk to the next until the right authority finds an excuse to stamp it out.

"If you choose to join there will be a test, of course--" again his eyes swept her face appraisingly, "but I think you will pass. You have the look of someone with a sharp mind that's been drowned in too much paper, not a complete incompetent." He chuckled. "God knows you've got the spark of Justice in you, given that stunt that brought you here. You'll have to interrogate three prisoners to show us how you think. You'll determine the veracity of the charges against them, and enact the appropriate punishment."

When he finished speaking he settled back into his chair, evidently expecting a slew of questions.

Rivka didn't so much as take a breath. There was nothing to ask, really. The man had said it all, and her choice was already made. However frightening the concept of hybrid Ranger-Magistrates, any chance of joining them was far better than being sent to Jhiordaan from which the only respite was death. Or maybe they'd return her to the planet and execute her.

The prison planet option had only been in her vivid imagination. No one else had said she was going there.

She closed her eyes and collected her thoughts.

"I would love to meditate on this issue, but the fact that I've never meditated before could be a hindrance to a successful outcome. I suspect you won't give me time to study appropriate techniques under a guru?"

He started to chuckle, shaking his head.

"I thought as much, but figured it wouldn't hurt to ask. Upon contemplation of my fate and in consultation with my buddy karma, I have decided to accept your offer—with certain conditions, of course."

He raised one hand and held up his middle finger. She laughed and raised her shackled hands to return his gesture. "I think I might like this side of the law," Rivka said.

The man pulled a key from his pocket and removed her shackles.

"You aren't worried that I might try to escape?"

"What the hell for and how? On this side of the law, as you so aptly put it, people try to escape from us, not the other way around."

She rubbed her wrists and rolled her shoulders.

"Let's get those tests done, Barrister." He extended a calloused hand. "And then I'll welcome you to the team. If you're still with us, that is."

4

Rivka walked with her head held high as she followed her unnamed benefactor, even though she still wore prison garb. He didn't seem interested in offering her new clothes, so she didn't bother asking.

"What's your name?"

"How about you call me Grainger?" he replied.

Rivka fought against rolling her eyes. "Well, *Grainger*, I see that you're no stranger to danger."

"Is that the best you have, Barrister? I may have to revise my opinion of you and your abilities."

"I'm just getting warmed up."

"Save it for the perps," Grainger advised warmly.

"You haven't exactly caught me at my best."

He looked down at her. "Holy crotch goblins, you look like an inmate. Right turn, *harch!*" Grainger made a sharp right down a side passage, and two turns later he used his palm print to open a door that had no signage on it.

Rivka stopped at the doorway, refusing to go in. He saw

her hesitation. "You are safe with me, but you can't be sure until you are." He pulled a dress and a Magistrate's jacket from a standing wardrobe.

"Those clash," she told him.

He tossed her the jacket. "Makes no difference to me." She looked at the dress that he had laid over the back of a chair.

"Give me a minute."

He left the room, and she went in and closed the door. *Trusting, but he's right. Why would I try to run?* She quickly surveyed the place. There was nowhere to go. She threw her prison clothes on the floor and stood on them as she put on the dress. It was a little big, as if they'd had her size before her brief incarceration and hadn't anticipated that she would quickly lose a great deal of weight. She left her prison sandals on the floor, opting to go barefoot before wearing anything that reminded her of jail.

She opened the door to find the corridor beyond empty. "What the hell?" She hurriedly retraced their steps to find Grainger waiting in the main corridor. "Is everything I do going to be some kind of test?"

"Maybe. Maybe not." He looked over her head. "Not as far as *you* know, anyway."

She felt her middle finger quivering as if it had a mind of its own, ready to jump into action. He watched her wrestle with her thoughts for a moment before tipping his head in the direction they'd been going.

She needed to clear her mind for the upcoming test, so she focused on his back until it became a blur. As with any case, she would study the information she had, taking care to note any and all anomalies. Did the statements match?

What about timelines? Were the elements of the crime present, and what could be proven? But in this case, she would have to learn all of that from the interrogation of a single person.

"Will I see any materials regarding these cases before I interview the suspects?"

"No written materials, just a verbal brief. Here's your brief, counselor. Perp number one is accused of capital theft of a piece of artwork. There is a datapad you can access to ask specific questions regarding procedural issues and such, but your focus must be on the perp.

"The second case involves assault and battery. Open and closed case since the man has confessed."

Rivka held up one finger to interrupt the briefing. "Not so open and shut. I will be the final arbiter of Justice in his case."

"You will. The third case is capital murder. A Yollin. There's video," Grainger ended abruptly. "Here we are. Good luck. If you need anything... Well, don't need anything. This is *your* test, not mine."

Three interrogations. Three separate determinations of Justice, and then deliver the appropriate punishment.

He opened the door and a man within hastily rose from behind the table. He couldn't stand up straight because of his shackles. Grainger touched Rivka's arm, stopping her. She turned to find a key dangling between his fingers. "Your call about removing the shackles before, after, or never."

"You're not being unreasonable." She winked at the Magistrate. With a flair, she strode into the interrogation room, flipping the door closed behind her.

She motioned for the man to sit and tapped the datapad to see what she had access to. Rivka hoped that the man would start talking; establish a baseline she could use to ask other questions. Anything he had prepared for her would be of no value except telling her what seed he was trying to plant.

"I took it," the man admitted softly.

Rivka stopped accessing the pad but didn't look up.

"Didn't think it were worth that much. No way, Jose!" he blurted.

Finally Rivka met his gaze. His eyes were wild, like a trapped animal's. She looked at him without blinking, making him think she was peering into his soul. He rocked back and looked away.

"Capital theft means that the death penalty attaches. There are multiple elements to your crime. *Actus reus* has been satisfied since you just told me that you did it. The *mens rea*, the mental aspect of this crime, is that you intended to permanently deprive the owner of his property, which is valued in excess of one hundred thousand Federation credits. Since you tried to sell that painting, I believe the *mens rea* has also been satisfied. You intended to permanently deprive the owner of his property. How do you plead?"

"What?" The man pulled against his shackles. The wildness returned to his eyes. "I'm not pleading to any theft that kills me!"

"You've chosen 'no contest' then?"

"What the hell does that mean? This is a rail job. I'm being railroaded. Fuck off!" His voice rose to a high pitch as he approached hysteria.

"I think you need to settle the fuck down." Rivka glared at him.

He started to bounce up and down rattling his shackles against the eyelet to which they were attached. Rivka stood, leaned across the table, and punched him in the forehead, driving him into his seat. He glared as she slowly sat down.

"That's better. Let's take a good look." Rivka accessed the case file that Grainger had led her to believe didn't exist. She studied a picture of the painting's rightful owner, who looked like a bureaucrat. *We hate bureaucrats, don't we?*

"Ricciardo Domesta owns the painting. Let's see how he acquired it..." She tapped a few spots on the screen and mumbled to herself as she got lost tracing the painting's provenance.

She canted her head at the screen. "What made you steal this painting in particular?"

"I looked around. It seemed valuable, in a nice frame and all, and it was easy to get."

Rivka rubbed her chin. "Did you see any other artwork that looked valuable?"

"No. The other doors were locked. This one was in the hallway."

"Does that make any sense to you?" she asked.

The man's lip curled as he started to get angry. "You calling me stupid?"

"I make no accusations. I'm trying to get to the bottom of this, and you're not helping. The easy answer is for me to declare you guilty, which you are, and walk out. Some nice gentlemen will collect you and flush you out an airlock. That's the easy answer, and if you keep giving me shit you'll be out the airlock before you can say 'boo.'"

He leaned his head almost to the table so he could scratch his scalp with his rough and dirty nails. It made Rivka wonder how long the man had been in custody.

"I don't know how rich people live. It was the first house of that type I'd ever been in."

"How did you get in?" she wondered.

"I was at the bar having a drink. Just one, because I been down on my luck and all, then this butler type shows up all pissed off at his boss. He says it'd serve him right to get rolled."

Rivka was incredulous. "That was all it took?"

"Fuck, no! How easy do you think I am, lady?"

The Queen's Barrister bristled.

"He bought me a couple drinks, and next thing I know I'm in the house. Everything looks shiny and new, just like the song."

Rivka's mind had been drifting. She was thinking through the crime as if she were trying it in court. His statement caught her attention as if someone had physically tapped her head.

"How did you get into the house?"

He shook his head. "Can't 'member."

"So you say," Rivka replied, taking everything a suspect asserted with a grain of salt. They were incentivized to lie. But he *had* admitted to taking the painting.

"The doors in the hallway were locked. I assumed you tried them all before deciding to take the painting?"

"Yuppers. All locked and bolted; they wouldn't budge." The man raised his arm as much as he could with the shackles and flexed to show a larger than average bicep. Rivka shook her head and looked back at her datapad. She wasn't getting anywhere.

She activated the voice command override. "AI, I could use your help."

"I am Lexi Malachi at your service. How can I make you smile today?" a pleasant young man's voice asked.

Rivka and the perp looked at the datapad.

"I want to know the provenance of the painting on the screen, please. It's owned by a Mister Ricciardo Domesta."

"Working," the happy AI reported. "There's nothing I like more than answering questions, solving riddles, or getting to the bottom of a troubling conundrum."

"Just report when you can give me the chain of custody for at least two owners prior to Domesta." Rivka looked at the pad, but there was nothing new to see. She lifted her head and locked eyes with the suspect. "What was the man's name who bought you drinks?"

The perp shrugged.

"Did you ever see him outside of the one night in a bar?"

"Never before. Never after, although after was limited to the cops hauling my ass in here."

"Yours could be the worst one-night stand story I've ever heard. What did you do after you took the painting?"

"Went to the pawn shop to sell it."

Rivka rubbed her temples to ease the growing pain behind her eyes.

The man started pulling at his shackles again. "Settle down," Rivka ordered in a tired voice, finally feeling the ill effects of prison life. She wondered how much sleep she'd gotten as the lack thereof suddenly caught up with her.

"You and your types trussed me up like a prize bistok calf, serving me up for slaughter to feed to the homeless. Ain't that some crap? Well, lady, you can suck my balls!"

Rivka's eyes narrowed. She could feel the fire rising within, so she reached across the table and grabbed him by the throat. Images rushed into her mind. The man at the bar, a blackout, waking in a chair in the hallway, the only thing not nailed down was the expensive painting, a hole-in-the-wall resale shop, the painting getting destroyed when the police came for him, and then being led away in handcuffs.

She let go. "I believe you. Lexi, what have you found?"

"Working," the AI replied once again.

Rivka leaned back in her chair and crossed her arms to wait. The man started to look around frantically.

"Calm down," she told him for the third time.

"When in the history of all humanity has anyone calmed down because they were told to?" the man shouted in a hysterical voice. *"Let me go!"*

"You already admitted to the crime, and you understand that I am authorized to mete out punishment up to and including your execution. Are you in such a hurry for that to happen, or maybe we can wait a little bit longer and see if we have our facts straight?"

The man slumped into his chair, head hanging as he looked at the floor.

"Mister Domesta purchased the painting from the artist for five hundred credits eighteen months ago," Lexi reported. "He insured it for over one hundred thousand credits immediately thereafter, using an appraisal from an individual whom I believe is not real."

"What does that mean?" the perp asked.

"It means that the elements of the crime of which you have been accused have not been met. Stealing a painting worth five hundred credits is a misdemeanor, and a minor one at that. I've already punched you in the head, and I don't feel like doing it again. Do you promise not to steal?"

The man vigorously nodded, eyes wide and eyebrows raised to show his sincerity.

Rivka went around the table to unlock his shackles, and he jumped to his feet. The Queen's Barrister kicked him behind the knee and slammed him back into his chair.

"I'm not finished," she said calmly as she returned to her side of the table. "If I see you in here again it will not go well for you. Keep your nose clean, and don't accept drinks from strangers. And one final note, if it seems too good to be true, it is. Now, fuck off." She stabbed a thumb at the door. The man ran out.

She wondered where he'd go, since they were on a ship or a space station. She wasn't exactly sure.

"Lexi, issue a warrant for the arrest of Mister Ricciardo Domesta on felony insurance fraud. Use your research to build the case file to share with the local Magistrates."

A slow clap sounded from behind her. "Looks like you're one for one, although I have to question the oft-tried calm-the-fuck-down technique. Appealing to the wisdom of the perp has never worked. We're usually a little more hands-on, but hey…you may help us to see the errors of our ways," Grainger mused, leaning casually against the wall.

"I could use a shower, some chow, and a little sleep in a decent bed."

"Couldn't we all." Grainger crossed his arms, making no move to accommodate her.

She waited, as did he. She kicked back, putting her feet on the table and lacing her fingers behind her head.

"Nice try." He leaned away from the wall and started to walk out. Over his shoulder, he told her in a soft voice, "Perp number two will be in momentarily.

5

Rivka quickly stood, brushed her clothes straight. She'd forgotten that she was wearing a dress, the color of which didn't suit her, and the Magistrate's leather jacket. She liked the soft feel, and the emblem of the Magistrate's office was a small pin on the lapel.

The jingle of shackles came from the corridor beyond the open door. A man shuffled in, pushed roughly by the same guards who had escorted her a short while earlier. "Easy!" she ordered, using her authority. They nodded in unison, pushed the man one step farther into the interrogation room and closed the door behind them.

"Sit down, please." Rivka pointed to the recently vacated chair. Once he was in place, she sat down and accessed the datapad and the man's case file.

"I did it. I beat that guy within an inch of his life. If they hadn't pulled me off him, I might have killed him." The man's words were barely above a whisper, his eyes glistening as he delivered his own eulogy.

"Why did you do it?"

"He pissed me off, made me as angry as I've ever been."

"About what?"

The man shrugged. "It doesn't matter."

"They are just words, but they can hurt, can't they?" she said, showing empathy to get him to talk more.

"I did it. I beat him like a rented mule."

"Even a rented mule doesn't deserve to be beaten. Why did you do it?"

"He pissed me *off*," the man said, putting an inflection as if it were a question.

"Not good enough. We don't get to go around pummeling people, no matter how big of an asshat they may be." Rivka steepled her fingers before her, elbows on the table. The case file had been no help. It was three sentences stating that the perpetrator beat the victim.

"What did he say?" Rivka was curious, even though it was irrelevant to the case. They only needed the act, not the mental state, but that had been proven through his repeated confession.

The man shrugged again.

"Bullshit. You're covering for someone aren't you?"

"Say what?" The man looked confused.

Rivka watched his body language, which showed no subterfuge. Maybe he wasn't covering.

"What am I supposed to do with you?" she asked. "You seem to know more of what you need than I do. You understand the crime of which you're accused, and I expect you understand what kind of punishment you could be subjected to."

"You've got to lock me away from other people. I can't

be trusted around them. They make me angry sometimes, and I can't control it."

"Bullshit, you hick-ass dumb fuck!" she yelled, slapping the table and jumping to her feet. He rocked back in his chair. She hadn't hooked his shackles to the ring on the table. "What kind of chickenshit are you? You're an adult! Fucking act like it!"

"But I get angry," he whined.

"You look like a spoiled child who didn't get his way." She walked around the table and pushed him. With her touch, she felt his emotions surging. She balanced on the balls of her feet and pushed him again.

He roared and reached out, but his shackles held his hands back. Rivka turned away, continuing her momentum with a back kick to his stomach. He bounced off his chair and landed in the fetal position, cradling his mid-section.

Rivka straightened her clothes and returned to her seat. "Please sit down." She pointed to his chair.

He gingerly got to his feet and crawled slowly into his chair.

"If you had killed that man there would have been nothing I could have done for you, but you did not take that final and fatal step. I believe there is hope for you, so I am sentencing you to anger management and rehabilitation." She tapped on the datapad. "Lexi, please put the prisoner on probation and schedule him for daily anger management therapy."

"So let it be said, so let it be written, so let it be done," Lexi declared.

"Does that mean yes?" Rivka wondered.

"Mister Strathbourg has been scheduled. The times and directions will be included in the wrist monitor he'll wear at all times as part of his probation."

Rivka pointed a finger at the man. "Go forth and anger no more, my good man. When you find the root of your fury, you'll be able to douse it and take control of your life once again. Be excellent."

She unlocked his shackles, and they joined the first prisoner's set on the floor. The guards met him at the door and affixed an oversized device to his wrist. The pleasant voice of the AI greeted him. Lexi recited the man's schedule as they went down the hall until Rivka could no longer hear the AI's voice.

She tapped the datapad, trying to read the third case file before the final prisoner arrived.

"One left. Are you going to let him go too?"

"It would be ill-advised to make a decision without going through the process. The process works, if we only give it a chance," Rivka replied.

"Sounds like something a self-licking ice cream cone of a bureaucrat would say." Grainger relaxed on one leg with the other braced against the wall, leaning back with his arms crossed.

"The universe needs bureaucrats," Rivka countered, trying to get the Magistrate's goat.

"Like the universe needs pimples on its ass."

"The universe needs us, too—those who uphold and enforce the laws made by people wearing expensive clothes and looking down their noses at the ones who do their bidding. But we get to be more hands-on, did you say, in the laws we enforce? Stupid laws will die because they *won't* be enforced."

"And stupid bureaucrats will find themselves on the wrong end of Justice," Grainger snarled. His cheek muscles bulged as he clenched his jaw.

"What is the Magistrate's role in providing input to the bureaucrats?"

Grainger made fish lips at Rivka. "Your Yollin has arrived. Good luck. At the end of this one you'll get your shower and hot chow, but will it be as a Magistrate or as a prisoner? The jury is still out."

Rivka wanted to give him the finger, her automatic response to most of the things Grainger was telling her, but stopped as a shackled two-legged Yollin appeared in the doorway. He was taller than her and had a carapace. Mandibles extended from the sides of his head.

"Take your seat," she directed, pointing.

"I didn't do it," he snapped.

Rivka kept her face neutral and refused to answer him.

"Did you hear me? I said I didn't do it," the Yollin said loudly.

The door closed behind her. She looked at the datapad, one which the case file was already loaded. She tapped the link to the security footage. High definition video showed the Yollin before her driving a metal spike into another Yollin's head. After the victim fell, the attacker kicked the spike to drive it deeper, throwing his head back and laughing while he strolled casually away.

"Did you fucking hear me, dickface?"

Rivka raised one eyebrow. "Why did you do it?" she asked in a level voice.

"I didn't."

"Looks to me like you did."

"All Yollin look alike, but your stupid dickface can't see that. Jumping to conclusions, it's what dickfaces do."

"I am utterly appalled at your language and demeanor and by the violence with which you murdered that man. You did it, and I am your judge, jury, and executioner. What do you think about that, Yollin?" Rivka asked as the heat rose from her neck to her face.

"Dickface," the Yollin repeated. "I didn't do it."

Rivka forced her eyes back to the datapad. "Lexi, can you compile profile pictures for all Yollin within one kilometer of the murder site for the time period one hour prior to one hour after."

"Working," the AI acknowledged in its young male voice. She leaned back and crossed her arms. The Yollin was shackled, but not locked to the eyelet. He was much bigger than Rivka, his carapace scratched and scarred from a hard life. She wondered if Grainger was nearby in case this Yollin decided to take matters into his own hands. His mandibles clicked as he watched her.

"Dickface. I didn't do it," the Yollin repeated.

"Two legs. You're lucky the Yollin people allowed you to live, so substandard are you. Basically an animal among the real Yollin."

"If you are trying to provoke me, you'll have to try harder than that. I didn't do it, and won't give you the satisfaction of fitting me up for something else."

"I think you can fit yourself up just fine without my help."

"Done," Lexi reported. Four images filled the screen.

Rivka looked them over, then tapped to access the next four. Seventeen screens of Yollins.

"None of your people look alike. More importantly, there were only three with two legs in the area all night."

"One of the other two must have been the killer. All I know is that it wasn't me."

"There's the rub, dickface," Rivka started. "The other two were females. It was you, all right."

"Bullshit! I didn't do it!" the Yollin huffed, and grunted his dismay. He clicked his mandibles in annoyance, opening them wide as Yollins did to intimidate an opponent.

"Bullshit. You did it." Rivka glowered at him. She didn't know why she didn't feel the need to dig deeper. She'd made her decision. Was Grainger right in thinking she would decide too quickly?

"Why am I being judged by humans? I demand a Yollin court!"

"Shut your pie hole. I need to think." Rivka flipped from screen to screen reading the statements, watching the video, and looking through the images of the other Yollin. She didn't find anything that suggested a different course of Justice, but she had one other trick up her sleeve.

She leaned forward to study the Yollin, and he moved toward her and growled. She lashed out with her hand and grabbed him by the wrist and he tried to grab back, but he was too slow. His shackles caught as she pulled him sideways.

His darkness invaded her mind and tore at her soul, and she gasped as she released her grip. Spittle flew toward her when the Yollin spread his mandibles wide and roared.

There was fire in front of her eyes. She jumped up and, twisting like a gymnast, drove both feet into the Yollin's chest. With a crack and snap, he flew backward, hit the wall, and slumped to the floor.

She was over the table in an instant, flying through the air with her knees tucked to her chest. She stomped hard as she came down on the Yollin's chest with all the fury in her body.

The crack echoed through the small room. Rivka staggered off the prisoner's chest, and he gurgled for a moment before exhaling his final breath. His eyes started to glaze.

The door to the room opened, and Grainger rushed in. He didn't need to bend down to see that the Yollin was dead, his carapace cracked and driven into his organs.

"What did you do?" he demanded, his face grim, and she gaped. It had happened again—she'd lost control after seeing the horror within another creature.

Rivka closed her mouth as she recovered her wits. The fury faded, and she brushed her clothes off and straightened herself. "The evil in that one would have tainted anyone he touched. The universe is better without him in it." She lifted her chin defiantly.

Grainger's scowl turned to a smile as he extended a hand. "Welcome to the team."

"That's it?" Rivka's lip curled of its own accord. "You bastard!"

"What did I do? If I had an ex-wife, I think she'd sound just like you." He pulled his arm back. "You don't get to shake my hand."

"What?" Rivka looked at the empty space between them as if a hand would materialize any second.

"Come on. Chow, a hot shower, then rack time. You have an appointment with the Pod-doc first thing tomorrow. You showed some strength in there, but that's not enough. Not all perps are cuffed."

Grainger signaled to the guards.

"Dispose of this garbage," he instructed them, pointing at the corpse without looking at it.

"Yes, Magistrate," the one replied.

"Collect those shackles and put them where they can be used again," Rivka added, trying to assert some authority.

"Yes, Magistrate," the other replied.

Grainger left without a further glance. Rivka hurried after him. "Wait, I have questions..."

6

Rivka woke with a start. She didn't know the time or where she was. She bolted upright, looking around as she tried to get her bearings.

"Lights," she called. Her room slowly illuminated. It was a single with all the amenities of any hotel room, but she wasn't in a hotel. She was on a space station in orbit over a planet where she'd had a budding career as a barrister. That had ended when she became a murderer.

And her new career had begun—in space. She had become a Magistrate. Beyond a barrister, more than one who argued the law. She was judge, jury, and executioner, and she'd already carried out her first execution with extreme prejudice.

She hadn't been wrong. She'd seen into the nightmare that was his dark soul. Would that hold up in court?

"It doesn't have to," she told the empty room. Rivka got up, went to the sink, and splashed water on her face before taking a long drink. The little things. Yesterday she had been a prisoner. "What the hell have I gotten myself into? Uphold the law, but use voodoo tricks to do it?"

The Yollin probably would have been convicted. The video had been convincing, but his denial would have carried weight with many juries. Criminals loved to confess. What they didn't know is that most would get off if they simply denied everything and gave the prosecution nothing to work with. Forensics were limited, and there was always contamination.

But not in the soul of the accused.

"What is happening to me?" she asked, but no one answered. She was alone and the clock said she was up too early, but it was too late to get any meaningful sleep. She decided another shower was in order, along with a cup of coffee. The room's hot water dispenser turned the dehydrated crystals into a cup of joe. She winced when it first hit her tongue but decided that for its therapeutic value it was good enough.

Grainger had improved his estimate of her size, based on how well everything in her wardrobe fit. It was like she had acquired her own personal concierge. She dressed casually in jeans and a stylish off-the-shoulder shirt. She started to walk out, but stopped. Her Magistrate's jacket was hanging over one of two chairs at a small table. Rivka liked how it felt.

And the status—it screamed "Magistrate" loud and proud. She wrapped herself in the jacket and headed out the door to learn more about the station that would apparently be her training ground.

Corridors upon corridors and levels upon levels. Rivka hadn't known that such a place existed. When she finally found an external wall, she looked through a small window at the planet below. So close, yet so far away.

Why? she wondered. *Seeing the guilty for what they really are and meting out Justice—I can see why the Rangers received a bad rap.* It would be easy for those without the responsibility to envy those with it, but for most, the burden of Justice would be too great.

A Magistrate's life.

She took in her surroundings, the space station and its people. There was nothing else. There was nothing natural about living in space. The people kept the station alive and the station kept the people alive, and together they did more than survive. The bustle and the energy—they were hope. She hadn't known what it was like to be without hope until she'd been jailed. Rivka took a deep breath. Free air smelled good, even if it *was* recycled.

She looked at her datapad. Time to meet Grainger.

Rivka strolled down corridors and up levels with a sense of purpose. She found the door, knocked, and entered without waiting to be admitted.

Inside, she found a cross between a weight room and a dojo. Grainger was sitting on a bench, sweat running down his head and a towel wrapped around his neck.

"You just come flouncing in here like you own the place?"

"I don't flounce," Rivka shot back, putting her hands on her hips in defiance. "Wait, how do you define flounce?"

"Sashay with plenty of sass."

"If I could do that I would, but I can't so I don't—although I'm not above trying. Wait, how do you define sashay?"

"So this is how it's going to be, huh?"

"Have to have shared definitions if any conversation is going to move forward."

Grainger smacked his lips slowly and pointed to a locker. "Get dressed. It's workout time."

"I thought I was going into the Pod-doc..." His look silenced her. She headed for the locker to find that there was no privacy, only a shower behind them where they changed in the open.

"What's the problem, Magistrate?" Grainger asked, turning back to the weights and adding two plates to the stack.

"Nothing," she mumbled. She carefully hung her jacket, removed the rest of her clothes, and tossed them in. She put on her gi and wrapped the annoyingly white belt around her waist, cinching it tight. She turned back, expecting Grainger to be watching, but he wasn't. He was breathing in rhythm with his repetitions, his muscles bulging with his efforts.

He finished his set and cleared the bench, using his towel to wipe up the sweat.

"How long have you been here?"

"How long were you flouncing around the station?"

"Probably as long as you've been here, but the world is out there. And I think we've already established that I don't flounce."

"Says you. If we don't train in here, we won't be ready for what's out there. You have to be smarter, faster, and stronger than any person or creature you come up against. And most of the time, criminals run in gangs. You don't come up against just one. You get to fight the whole fucking mob of them."

Grainger pulled up his shirt to show a buff and tanned body with a rock hard six-pack. Rivka wasn't sure what she was supposed to be looking at.

"Here," he said with a snort, pointing to a faded line across his chest. She leaned closer and saw a number of lines. Some wrapped under his arm to cross his back.

"What happened?"

"A gang that got the smart idea that we were vulnerable to silver, so they silver-plated all their shit."

"Silver? How is that possible? Are you a Were?" she asked in a rush.

"Yes. Silver cuts through the nanocytes that course through my blood. Hurts like a motherfucker, and leaves one hell of a mark." He pointed to the smooth skin around her neck and on her arms. "You'll get your own scars. Pod-docs can't fix everything. And anyone carrying a silver weapon? That's cause for arrest and on-the-spot judgment. Those fuckers are out to hurt someone from the Federation."

He removed most of the plates from the bench-press machine and motioned for Rivka to lie down. She took her place, lifting her feet to the bench instead of straddling it. She tested the weight and then started the set. The first three weren't too bad, but after that she ran out of power quickly. The seventh rep never happened. She pushed at the bar balanced across her chest, but nothing moved besides a single vein that started throbbing in her forehead.

She hadn't even broken a sweat.

"You've got some work to do, Lightweight," Grainger told her with a scowl.

"How did you do on your first day?"

"My first day doesn't compare to yours. I was already Ares, God of War on mine. Your *best* day will not be as good as my first day." He stared her down.

"Holy shit!"

He started to laugh. "Just kidding. On my first day I was a total lost cause, just like you are, Lightweight."

"Take your 'Lightweight' and shove it up your ass!"

"I don't want you up my ass."

"What!" She rolled off the bench and came to her feet, fists raised.

"You don't want to do that."

"I clearly don't have your respect, so maybe a little girl slapping you right in your mouth will change your attitude." She waited for him to blink before lashing out. Her hand barely left her side before a sledgehammer of a fist hit her in the forehead. Rivka went down like a jumble of bricks.

"You have my respect. What you *don't* have is my experience or training, dumbass." He walked toward the lockers, his gi dropping on the deck before he reached the shower. He slung his towel onto a hook before ducking under the water.

"You are a strange man," Rivka mumbled. She closed her eyes and willed the pounding in her head to go away. "What have I gotten myself into?"

"Would you look at those knuckle marks? Epic, my man, epic," the technician said while studying Rivka's forehead.

"Sometimes training is hard." Grainger leaned close, stifling a snort. "And realistic."

"Into the Pod-doc with you," the technician ordered.

Rivka undressed and climbed into the device. The case closed and the AI started to work its magic. It sampled her DNA and started to program the nanocytes to make Rivka's body stronger and heal itself faster; help her do all the things she could do already, but orders of magnitude better.

"Did she want to be taller?" the technician asked.

"Sure. Plus her up a little," Grainger replied. "Anything else?"

"I've got it from here. It'll take a few hours to grow her bones and add muscle mass without too much pain and anguish."

The Magistrate reached the door and stopped. He spoke over his shoulder. "Give her something fantastic to change how she sees herself. Maybe the eyes. Give her eyes like no one else's." Grainger chuckled as he walked away.

"Will do, boss." The technician browsed the database, securing the door to the chamber before accessing restricted sites. Pornstars had a proclivity for the extreme. He pulled up a few—cat's eyes, single-color eyes—and then there they were, simple yet exotic: a golden-blue hazel with oversized irises. He input the settings for those, and also added a greatly improved ability to see in the dark. "Pretty eyes that are functional, although they *are* like someone else's. They'll never find out about Midnight Sass."

Vered sat in the small coffee shop, his back to the flimsy partition that acted as a wall between the restaurant and a women's accessory store. He watched people walking by, examining them quickly to determine whether they were a threat or not. Some saw it as a game. It had become so ingrained in his being that it simply *was*.

Personal security for the rich and famous wasn't something anyone could turn off, even if the current clientele were neither rich nor famous.

The large man looked out of dark brown eyes from beneath a heavy brow. He had caramel-colored skin with jet black hair, all of which came from a melting pot of ethnic influence—exotic beauty in a seductive man-candy package. He was the hired muscle, assuming he could get hired. He had arrived early for his interview. This was just another client, but this time it was for long-term employment, not the usual one-off.

He nursed his coffee as he waited for his potential employer.

A man wearing the jacket of a Magistrate walked casually through the common area. His eyes bored into Vered's, and they sized each other up as the distance between them closed. Vered stood, even though he didn't want to. He was willing to be less dominant when looking for a job. Once he was hired, he'd take control to keep his client safe.

He'd get paid because they would survive as they always did, but inevitably he'd piss off the wrong person and be casually let go.

I need to up my game. Maybe having a Magistrate as a client would give me the culture chops. He laughed at the thought.

Grainger stopped before him with a curious expression on his face, and Vered sobered as the two men shook. Each gripped tightly, and the contest was on. Grainger smiled as he applied pressure, and Vered grimaced when the bones in his hand started to grind together. He bowed his head, and each released his grip.

Vered rubbed the circulation back into his hand. "You don't look like you have the guns, but I have to give it to you."

"Give what to me?" Grainger asked innocently.

"That you're stronger than me. But I have other skills, too."

"And that's what we're here to talk about, Vered. May I call you Red?" Grainger pulled the chair out and sat down.

"That's my preferred nickname, so sure—especially if it'll give me bonus points to get me hired."

"I already know about you. I want to hire you, but you better be sure you want the job. You should be interviewing me, not vice versa."

"Vice? Are they here? I haven't juiced in a long time, but I still don't like answering questions from cops."

Grainger stared open-mouthed. He composed himself and explained, "I want to hire you as a bodyguard for a new Magistrate. She needs to be constantly training in hand-to-hand combat. You'll find that she's unnaturally strong." Grainger stretched his fingers out and curled them back into fists. "She has a nice ship waiting for her that she has yet to learn about, and she'll travel the galaxy to adjudicate various legal issues. It'll probably be a month before she goes out on her own. Between now and then you'll partake of all the physical training she does, and you'll watch out for her while she's on this station."

"Sounds too easy. You're going to pay me to work out?"

"I'm going to pay you to help *her* work out, but you're going to need to get stronger…and probably faster, too. You will have nothing to do with her legal work, but you will need to watch her back while she is embroiled in the law."

"I have to babysit?"

"Yesterday she killed a Yollin with her bare hands." Grainger put his elbows on the table and rested his chin on his hands.

"A Yollin? It's a start, but I'll reserve judgment. I would like the job if you'll have me. I can watch out for one of your legal people. Lawyers, the fungus that grows on the slime of the universe." After the words had come out he slapped a hand over his mouth, but it was too late.

Grainger thumped the big man on his bulky shoulder. "No sweat, I don't like lawyers either. You'll see that we're a little bit different in what we do. There's probably going to be a bit more hands-on than you would expect. As Magistrates we not only defend clients, we mete out Justice."

"Sounds like you're the judge and executioner."

"We'd like to think we're fairer than that. Judge, *jury*, and executioner." Grainger removed a datapad from his coat. "Here's our arrangement in writing. Please have your lawyer review any contract before you sign."

Red held out his thumb. Grainger scrolled to the end where the bodyguard affixed his thumbprint in lieu of a signature, having not read a single word.

"Don't fuck it up," Grainger advised. "You don't have to worry about getting sued for breach of contract. You'll need to worry about getting killed. As of right now, you need to bring your 'A' game."

"That's the only game I got, Mister."

7

The lid on the Pod-doc raised, and Rivka blinked rapidly to clear her vision. The room had been darkened—she knew it had—but everything was in vivid focus. She sat up slowly and the technician handed her a robe, but she didn't put it on.

"It'll take a little while to get used to the new you."

"How much changed?" she croaked, reaching for a jug of water nearby. She drank the whole thing.

"You're five centimeters taller, about fifteen kilos heavier, and your eyes are a different color," the technician replied in a neutral voice.

"Fifteen kilos?" Rivka stood up, growling as she fought to gain her balance. She looked at her new body. "Holy shit."

She ran her hands over her still-lean form. "I don't see fifteen kilos."

"Your muscles are far denser now. You'll have to get

used to those so you don't accidentally break stuff. Hold out your hand."

She showed her left hand, palm up. The technician dragged the point of a sharp blade across her palm.

"What the hell, jagoff?" she exclaimed, cradling her hand. As she watched, the blood stopped flowing and the skin knitted back together. The technician waited until she'd internalized what she'd just seen.

"The new you." He showed her to a mirror. She twirled a finger at him so he'd turn around and looked at herself in the buff before noticing her eyes. She leaned in close.

"What happened to my eyes?"

"Computer selection as an optimal enhancement. Your night vision is far beyond any normal human's capability. It rivals that of cats."

"Cats are optimal? Is that what I heard?"

The man shrugged. "At least the knuckle marks are gone from your forehead."

"At the very least, and thanks for the reminder. I may never live that down."

She put her clothes on. Her Magistrate's jacket was a touch tighter across the shoulders and her jeans were a little short, but everything would do. She tossed the robe across a chair and turned to leave.

The door opened, and Grainger walked in. "It's about time," he griped by way of greeting.

She threw up her hands and made a face at him.

"Come on. You need to get used to those big muscles before you break your head."

He waved at her to follow. She casually walked up behind him and gave him a hard push, and he stumbled forward. "Not bad, lightweight." He headed out the door and turned left.

They walked in silence until they reached the unlabeled area she thought of as the Magistrates' gym. There was a large man already there.

"Say hi to Red, your personal bodyguard, then get dressed. Weights followed by sparring."

"I have a bodyguard? What the hell for?" She looked sharply at the man, who closed his eyes and started a new set on the military press machine.

"Don't ask me, I'm the hired muscle."

"Because you need to focus on the law. He'll make sure no one sneaks up behind you." Grainger faced his locker as he dressed. "Do you understand what you're getting into? We don't deal with white-collar crime or petty criminals. That Yollin yesterday? He's on the weak-sister end of where we go. Get it into your head that the entire law-breaking universe is better off if you're dead."

He faced her, jaw set.

"You're not kidding."

"About something like that? No, unfortunately not. At least I don't have to see their evil like you do with your gift, if you can call it that. Maybe it's your curse, but it has brought you to the ranks of the Magistrates. For that, I'm thankful."

"I don't even know what we do," Rivka admitted. She sat on a bench and frowned at the floor.

"In due time, Lightweight. Hey, would you look at that?" Grainger pointed to the bench press.

Rivka followed his finger and shook her head.

"Those weights are not lifting themselves. Get dressed.

Those weights need you to save them from a boring life of proving that gravity exists."

"You are a strange man," Rivka reiterated as she put on her gi.

Grainger smiled and nodded to the corner. "Changing room."

"Has that been here this whole time?"

He shrugged and joined Red to throw some serious tonnage around. Rivka took the bench and started light. After nearly launching the bar through the ceiling, she added six plates, then four more. She giggled as she powered through weight she'd never imagined she could lift. She finally flipped the lever for the entire stack. She gritted her teeth and grunted. Gravity held it back, but her new power took over. It started slowly moving upward.

"You might want to take it easy..." Grainger cautioned.

The tendon snapped with a sound like a balloon popping. The weight stack crashed to the bottom of the slots, and the bar slammed down hard centimeters from Rivka's chest. She howled in agony.

"Don't think you're getting out of sparring," Grainger warned her.

She looked at him through features contorted with pain. "How will that be possible?"

"Give it five minutes. I expect your nanocytes are already racing to your injury and they'll have you right as rain. You need to build your physical mass more through exercise before you try to lift the whole world. The nanocytes give you greater strength, but they also give you a greater belief in your ability. The Pod-doc gave you fifteen kilos of more dense muscle, but it isn't ready to go all-out. You'll spend the next month building up so you'll be ready."

Rivka rubbed her elbow. The pain was lessening with each passing moment.

Grainger stretched. "Since we have a little time before you get back to it, here's your schedule. Five in the morning, chow. Then weights and sparring. By nine am, more chow. After that, back to school, Magistrate. Noon is lunch. After lunch, more sparring, this time using regular and improvised weapons. Then chow, then more class, dinner, and firing range. The evenings are yours to do whatever you want. That will start around eight."

"I have nine hours to myself each night? Generous. And what's with all the food? I'll get fat."

"You're on the crash course. One month to both get in shape and become self-sufficient as a Magistrate. You will *not* get fat. The nanos will draw most of their energy from your body, with alternate power coming from the Etheric dimension. You won't get fat, even if you grow lazy—as lightweights are wont to do."

"Me, lazy? I'm pretty sure that won't happen." She flexed the bicep of her undamaged arm. "I like what I see." She turned back to Grainger and fixed him with a serious expression. "I know what the alternative would have been for me—death or imprisonment on Jhiordaan. You've given me a new lease on life, so don't think me ungrateful."

"Show your gratitude by doing a good job, Lightweight." Grainger waved at Red to join Rivka. "Make sure she stays on the training regimen, as in, no more exploding tendons."

"Can I get some of those nano-things?" the large man asked.

"No." Grainger started a yoga routine, twisting his body and holding the position through a number of slow breaths.

Rivka faced Grainger, fists up. Red adjusted her stance, moving her feet closer together and tucking her elbows in.

Grainger waved her forward, and she moved in. Red stopped her and adjusted her position again. "If you keep your feet too wide you can't adjust quickly enough. If you keep your elbows out, you expose your ribs and weaken your strikes because you have less leverage." Grainger nodded at the bodyguard approvingly.

She waded in and started flailing, and Grainger blocked every blow. When they were tangled up, she drove a knee upward. He turned his body and knocked her knee away with his, then twisted her around, wrapping her with her own arm and slamming her face-first into the mat.

He backed away and assumed his ready position.

Red picked her up off the floor as one would a child and deposited her on her feet. Even with her extra fifteen kilos, she was nothing to the big man.

"What did you do wrong?" Grainger asked between his raised fists.

"Overexposed. Less leverage because of shorter arms."

"Your physical size is never a shortcoming, because it won't change. Don't ever look at your body as something that's wrong. It's simply what you have to work with. Your advantage is that you are a smaller target, so you'll have to get close to an opponent. We'll help you figure out how to make that work for you."

Rivka nodded and powered in for round two.

By round seventeen, she lay on her back where she had fallen. "I feel like shit."

"Time to recharge those overworked nanocytes." Grainger walked to his locker and got dressed.

"Could you at least have the grace to sweat?" Rivka mumbled. She rolled to her stomach and pushed up, then swayed on her weak legs. She went to the shower and closed her eyes as she let the hot water run over her. She heard a noise and looked into the training room to find Grainger beating the crap out of Red. She grabbed her towel and rushed over.

Red held up his hands in surrender, and Grainger let the man up. The anger on the Magistrate's face was clear, but faded quickly with the bodyguard's submissive pose.

"Nothing to see, just finish and let's go. I'm hungry."

The bodyguard backed away and went to his locker, then sniffed under his arm. "Do we have time for me to get a quick shower, sir, ma'am?"

"We do," Rivka answered instantly, watching Grainger for a clue. He gave nothing away. She took her clothes into the changing room. By the time she was finished Red had showered and was getting dressed.

The three left together, Rivka and Grainger side by side and the bodyguard following at a distance, where he could intervene if they were attacked while giving them their privacy.

"I suppose you'll tell me what that was all about?" Rivka whispered.

"Somebody spent a little too long watching something he didn't need to be watching."

"So you're my protector, too?"

"I'm training both of you. He needs to watch for threats, no matter how much skin you flash. You two will be working closely together. He has his job, and that's to protect you; nothing more. There can *never* be anything more."

"Not my type," Rivka said, glancing over her shoulder at the hulking man behind them.

"He now knows that beyond a shadow of a doubt. He'll be a good member of your team."

"Oooh! I get a team?"

"Do you think this is the Wild West? We aren't sending Magistrates to the frontier with a gun and a prayer. You're going to get a state-of-the-art combat ship with an Entity Intelligence, an EI."

"I didn't hear the word 'sidekick.' I'm feeling put out."

"Okay, Batman. You're just going to have to work without a sidekick, like the days before Robin."

"Crushing my dreams. I always wanted to have a Robin." Rivka twisted her mouth from side to side.

"Bah! He was more trouble than he was worth. It's Alfred you really want backing you up." Grainger nodded at his analogy.

"I'm going to have to contemplate that in my free time."

"You'll need less sleep now, if you haven't already guessed. We're halfway through today's schedule. Afternoon chow, then legal training. The AI is set up to run you through the legal wringer."

"Chow? Such an unappealing word. As lawyers, we should have a finer command of language. Breakfast, second breakfast, elevenses, lunch, afternoon tea, dinner, evening meal, and snacks. Why do you call everything chow?"

"Military training, and because it is. Don't glamorize the chow until you see it, counselor."

"I can't simply call it 'chow' because of one witness. I shall reserve judgment until I see it for myself. I shall call it a late lunch for now."

"Touché."

8

The first two weeks passed at glacial speed but the last two weeks flew by. Rivka was getting antsy. She raced through her reps and stood with her hands on her hips, waiting for Red to catch up. He finished and stood, stretching out his muscles while he scanned the room, left to right, up and down, the way he'd checked out every room they'd entered. His eyes barely ever rested on Rivka.

Grainger had trained him well. Better, he had taken the training as a professional and applied it to his daily routine.

"What are they paying you?" she asked.

He pulled his right arm over his head to ease the pressure on his lats. "You don't know?"

"No. As a matter of fact, I don't know what they're paying me, either. Hey! What are you paying us?"

"Need to know, and you don't."

"I don't need to know what you're paying me?" she asked.

"He doesn't need to know what you're being paid, and you don't need to know what he's being paid. No one needs to know what I get paid. You know what they say, don't you?"

"I'm not sure I want to even try."

"Ignorance is bliss."

"No, it isn't!" she retorted. "You're not going to tell me, are you?"

"I think it's time that we go see your corvette. It arrived a few days ago."

"When the fuck were you going to tell me that?"

Grainger looked shocked. "Just now. Damn, Magistrate, sometimes you ask questions that add zero value to the conversation. I'm not sure there's enough time in all the universe to help you with that foible."

"I may not have many foibles, but they are magnificent," Rivka countered. "But I have a corvette. I guess I make good money, then."

Grainger stopped what he was doing. "The *Federation* has a corvette and suggests you don't damage it. Should you do so, you'll be an indentured servant for the remainder of your days as you hope in vain that your paltry pay will one day cover the cost of your egregiousness."

"It's called indemnification, and that clause is in my Magistrate package. If the poor corvette gets a boo-boo, it's in the line of duty. *Indemnified*, bitches. The Federation will cover it. Don't bluff a bluffer."

Grainger clasped his hands together and bowed deeply. "That, grasshopper, is your final test. Into the universe with you. Go forth and do great things in the name of

Justice. Your chariot to the gods awaits."

She gave him the finger.

When he stood his hands were unclasped, the middle fingers of each hand touching, the other fingers folded back. The classic double-bird.

"And I *still* don't know what I get paid. If I try to buy lunch somewhere will my card be rejected?"

Grainger shrugged and gave her a half-smile. "Some lessons are best learned first-hand."

"I used to like you," she replied as they each chuckled at the humor of it. Red went into the corridor first before allowing the Magistrates to pass.

SOP that Rivka couldn't take for granted. She was getting ready to deploy on her first mission and had no idea what to expect. Her nerves were on edge.

"You need to go somewhere and do something. Your coat still smells new. It looks new, too."

"It'll get broken in soon enough," she replied.

Grainger shook his head and removed his Magistrate's jacket. "Here."

"That's yours."

He rolled his eyes. "You are a master at stating the obvious." He pushed the jacket toward her until she had to take it or stumble forward with it draped over her face. He snapped his fingers and pointed to her jacket.

They stopped while she changed. His was as soft as butter and a little big, but not as voluminous as she would have expected. She'd thought it would hang on her like a bag. It was faded just enough, and smelled of something that she couldn't place. It carried the small pin she had on her jacket. Grainger put it on. Hers looked too small on him, but she figured no one would say anything.

"Thanks," she mumbled.

"As you so succinctly stated, that jacket is *mine*. I'm giving this one to the cleaners. They'll give it that weathered look you desire."

"'I desire.' Interesting. I desire Justice for the universe, and you know what else? I desire my nanos to fix this broken tooth you gave me yesterday."

"Let me see," he demanded, and bent down to look into her mouth. She pointed with her tongue.

"No shit. That shouldn't happen. I'm going to talk with the Pod-doc technician. You go see a stomatologist and get that taken care of. You can't deploy with a bad tooth. How will you eat your chow?"

"No way! This isn't a disease, just a chipped tooth." Rivka waved off her mentor and shook her head. "I think a dentist will be fine. And for the record, the only way to stomach the chow is by shoveling it in. Does my corvette have a chef and real food?"

Grainger started to laugh. Unable to speak, he stumbled away.

She went to a nearby monitor and tapped the screen. "Please direct me to the nearest dentist."

"Doctor Toofakre is one level down."

"Doctor Toothacher? Come on, be serious."

"Toofakre." The AI displayed the spelling on the screen.

"Is there anyone else?"

"Doctor Payne is on the other side of the station."

"Toothache or pain, pick your poison. I'll give Toofakre a shot. If he hurts me, well, I'll make him feel it."

The barrister took the stairs down, preferring not to be trapped in an elevator. She wasn't a fan of strangers, and even less of being confined in a tight space with them. Red was with her, but she didn't have to put up with others.

When she reached the next level, she saw the sign—a big picture of a tooth. Just the thought of it made her mouth hurt, but she had already cut her tongue once on the sharp edge. She didn't need to do it again. She committed and strode briskly to the door, and it opened as she approached.

"Magistrate Rivka, we were notified you were coming. We've been expecting you."

"For all of two minutes?" Rivka wondered if her fellow Magistrate had set her up.

"We were informed as soon as you asked, so yes—for all of two minutes. We don't get many celebrities, you see."

"I'm hardly a celebrity," she countered.

"But people of your station have nanocytes that usually repair the damage. For whatever reason, yours have not. Please come into the back and let's get you fixed up."

"Are you the dentist, Dr. Toofakre?"

"Yes, that's me. An unfortunate family name, but I'm Tyler Toofakre the Fifth. I don't have much choice."

"But you don't look like a dentist."

"How am I supposed to look?"

"I don't know, but you look like a normal person. You don't have any bodies hidden in the back, do you?"

Toofakre laughed and brushed his hair back from his forehead. "I'm afraid not. If I go to jail, it won't be for that."

"What will it be for?" She fixed him with her piercing gaze and lightly touched his arm. In her mind she saw flashes from his life, but no crimes. Looking into someone's mouth, watching a movie, playing a video game, and drinking a beer with dinner.

"For being too boring, Barrister. I have to admit that I enjoy a life that's less exciting. It's nothing like yours. I suspect you chipped that tooth while bringing a criminal mastermind to Justice, delivering his punishment as he begged for mercy. Don't hurt me! Aha, Doctor Evil, your tidal wave of terror is over. You have crashed against the bulwarks of Justice!"

Rivka raised one eyebrow and contemplated going to Dr. Payne.

"Climb into the seat, and let's get that tooth of yours sorted so you can be on your way, keeping peace on the station and delivering Justice throughout the galaxy."

"I don't like pain in my mouth."

"That makes two of us. I have this pen-shaped syringe that makes it easy to deliver the anesthetic. You shouldn't feel a thing."

"I can't take you seriously as a dentist." Rivka held up a hand as the doctor leaned toward her, with his safety glasses firmly in place. The magnifying lenses had been flipped up, and he held his instruments steady a few fingerwidths from her mouth.

"Why not?"

"Because you look and act...*normal*."

"If you want Max Loony, you'll have to see Doctor Payne."

"So my choice is Toofakre or Payne?"

"Yes. Seems clear to me. Shall we?" The dentist motioned for her to open her mouth.

Rivka hesitantly complied. "But, *normal*," she mumbled as he went to work. Red stood against the wall with his arms crossed and watched the door.

The corvette was too big to fit in the small hangar bay of the station, even though it was only designed for a maximum of twelve crew and passengers.

Grainger led her to the top of the station, where a long access tube terminated at a closed airlock. As the group approached, it popped open and they walked through. The ship's hatch before them opened while the airlock door behind them closed. Grainger bowed and waved an arm toward the corvette. "Your ship."

Rivka hesitated only a moment before entering. She stopped and breathed deeply of the dry but clean recycled ship's air. She ran a finger over a horizontal surface and looked at it.

"I assure you, Magistrate, that the ship is immaculate. The air-handling system removes all of the dead skin and cat dander before returning oxygenated air back to you," a voice said over speakers placed throughout the ship. "Welcome aboard, Magistrate Rivka."

"Nice to be here, whoever you are."

"My sincere apologies, Magistrate. I'm Charles Woodworth the Third. Most people call me Chaz."

"Nice to meet you, Chaz. Let's have a look at how beautiful you are."

Vered cleared his throat. "Magistrate? Cat dander?"

"I heard it. I ignored it, since Grainger has accused me of stating the obvious. Clearly, there is a cat on board."

"I hate cats."

"What about dogs?"

"Dogs too. They're vermin, no better than rats. Can we have him removed?"

"Blasphemer!" Rivka shouted in an unusually loud voice, pointing one accusatory finger at her bodyguard. "We most certainly will not remove the cuddly kitty from the ship. We'll consider that little fuzzball as standard government Issue. Anything happens to him, he'll be replaced by two more. Do you understand?"

"Yes, but I don't like cats or dogs."

"That is a colossal improvement!" Rivka declared. "From hate to don't like. We'll take that as a win."

"But, but…" Red stammered.

"Carry on with the tour, Chaz."

"Yes, ma'am!" the EI replied. He walked the group to the bridge first to wow them with the technology.

"Nice, Chaz, but we don't have to fly the ship, do we?"

"I will fly the ship for you, but you can fly it too, if you wish."

"Maybe someday, but today is not that day. Nor is tomorrow, for that matter." Rivka looked at Red. "Do you fly?"

He pointed at himself with both hands and shook his head. "If I'm flying the plane, who's guarding the client?"

"I might suggest that if you're flying the ship, the client doesn't need to be guarded."

"Client always needs guarding. You leave that part to me and flying the ship to your new bestest buddy."

"That's me," Chaz replied. "I shall fly the ship while you partake of your human concerns. Next stop, the mess deck slash recreation room slash living room slash anything not sleeping or flying room."

"Do I hear you saying that there are cabins for sleeping, the bridge, and one other space on board this tub?"

"There is a storage area as well, but that's filled with stuff that needs to be stored."

"Lead on, kind EI." Rivka made big eyes at Grainger.

He yawned. "But it's a corvette."

"Sounds sexy until you get in," Rivka replied. The mess deck was open, with various elements that could be extended and retracted, like a table with bench seats. Six recliners were tucked into the side bulkhead. They folded out to face a wall screen on the opposite side. A weight bench could be raised from the deck. There was a single bar and no weights.

"What the hell am I supposed to do with this?" Red asked, picking up the bar.

"It's magnetic," the EI replied. The bar was yanked toward the metal deck, taking Red with it. It hit and stuck. The rings on each end kept his hand from being pinned underneath. He picked himself up from the deck, looking around sheepishly.

"I guess we'll try to make that work," Red said softly.

The kitchen contained a food processing unit and one drink station. "This is for twelve people?"

"It will service twelve people without any problems."

"As only an EI can say it. If there were twelve people squeezed aboard this thing, there would be problems. By the way, what's her name?"

"Federation Corvette Seven Seven Four."

"That's a hull number. What's her *name?*" Rivka pressed.

Grainger shook his head. "Looks like we get to name her."

Red pointed at Rivka. "*You* get to name her. I don't give an upside-down flying goat-fucking nut roll whether this tin can has a name."

"I'll take care of it. I can't have my baby without a name. Maybe Lucretia."

"Two seconds ago you were hating on your ride and now she's your baby?"

"Yes. It's just how things are going to be. Oh, Chaz, darling, lead me to the luxury Magistrate's suite, please."

"Prepare for disappointment." Grainger wouldn't look at her.

"Buzzkill," she shot back.

"Down the corridor. There are six cabins on the port side."

"I thought this ship could carry twelve people?"

"Now she's starting to get the picture."

"Everyone doubles up? The barbarity of it all. You'd think The Queen's Magistrate would be treated better. I'll have to send Bethany Anne a personal note stating my dismay."

Grainger raised one eyebrow. "I doubt the Queen will have any sympathy. You get a cabin to yourself. Stop whining and cradle your baby to your bosom."

Rivka gave Grainger a five-second stink-eye. Red squeezed past the Magistrates and started opening doors. "These are better than my first apartment."

"How's that?" Grainger asked, staring without blinking at Rivka's golden-blue hazel eyes.

"No rats." He tossed his jacket in the last berth and opened the door to the small cargo storage area. A white cat with gray spots shot past him up the passageway and stopped when it saw the Magistrates, bouncing sideways with an arched back and hissing at Grainger.

Rivka bent down. "Who is this pretty kitty?"

The cat stopped hissing, and she scooped him up before he knew what hit him. She cradled him expertly, holding his claws at bay and tickling his neck until he started to purr. Red slammed the door to his cabin and worked his way back to the side hatch, where he stood vigil to make sure no other undesirables entered the corvette.

Grainger waved and headed for the exit.

"Where are you going?"

He rolled his eyes and threw his arms down in dramatic exasperation. "Not with you, clearly. The EI has your briefing." Grainger stood up straight and turned serious. "It's time to go, Magistrate. You've been training with me for a month, but you've been training to do this job your whole life. Now is the time to embrace your gift and use it for the good of the universe. You are licensed to judge innocence or guilt and mete out punishment. I know you don't take the job lightly, but take it you must, and now is the time."

He waved, nodded to Red as he passed, and yelled over his shoulder, "Chaz, take her to the Intripas System, best possible speed."

"Yes, Magistrate Grainger. I will Gate the ship from within the system. We should be at our destination in less than thirty minutes."

9

On the ship's main screen, a brownish-blue planet rotated beneath a heavily clouded sky.

"Looks serene, don't you think?" she asked.

"I wouldn't know," Red replied softly, not because he was evasive, but because he *didn't* know. He had no interest in aesthetics.

"What motivates you, Red?" Rivka asked while reviewing the case file.

"A good workout. The hot dancers at an All Guns Blazing bar. The usual stuff."

"That's not what I mean." She looked up from the screen. "What is your motivation to do what you do? You know, be a bodyguard?"

He turned toward the planet's image, but he wasn't looking at it. His eyes were unfocused as he stared and narrated as if he were talking to himself. "All my life I've been keeping people safe. I knew I wasn't smart enough to be a leader, but I'm smart enough to know that they can't do it alone. As a child, I was bigger and faster. That has value. I sold my services way back then and protected whoever could pay, bullies or bullied alike. Didn't matter to me."

"You've been a bodyguard your whole life? I guess it's true that sometimes a profession chooses you and not the other way around. If you don't mind me getting personal, what happened to all the money you've made along the way?"

"I do mind. I'm not a gambler or a big drinker, but it went somewhere that mattered to me."

"That's good enough for me. Sorry to intrude." Rivka returned to her file.

Red glanced at her from the corner of his eye. He didn't want to share that he had used his money to bail his mother out of a series of bad debts, and then she had died as soon as she was free. The whole affair had left him bitter, and the last thing he wanted was to talk about it.

Rivka flipped another page on her datapad and...Criminal Mischief? *Why the hell are they sending a Magistrate out here to deal with a misdemeanor?*

"Because the perp is the governor's daughter," Rivka remarked aloud. "They're sending me to deal with a family squabble. Ain't *that* some shit?"

Vered didn't reply. It wasn't his place to comment on legal matters, plus, he didn't think she was talking to him. She often talked to herself. It was the curse of the lonely.

"Since this is the first case and my chance to prove myself, I'll treat it just like anything else. We'll interview those involved, collect data, and make a ruling. Should there be punishment, I'll have to take care of that since I can't pass it to dear old dad. Should she go free, I better be able to explain *why* in words the general population will understand. Words that don't start with 'governor's daughter.' Yup. That's what they sent me here for. Thanks, Grainger. I won't let you down, and afterward I'll take the opportunity to call you creative names I have yet to come up with."

"We are entering orbit. Please secure yourselves in case something goes awry," the EI suggested.

"Will it?" Rivka wondered.

"It hasn't yet, but one can't be too careful."

Red took one of the three seats on the bridge that wasn't the captain's chair, which he had directed Rivka into because it had the best workstations and he could secure the bridge from the back. He wasn't sure what he was securing it from.

The corvette bumped across the upper atmosphere, and the screen faded out for a few moments as the ship's energy diverted to the heat shields. A miniaturized Etheric power supply propelled the small vessel and juiced her systems. It gave her the ability to Gate from one end of the universe to the other in a single jump. The power supply would change the Etheric Federation.

Rivka didn't think about any of that, just accepted that the ship took her where she needed to go. Although the ship had fantastic capabilities, she took it for granted. The one who had designed the systems and made them available would have been appalled.

The ship bounced back into a high-orbit, coming at the space station from below.

"Shall I coordinate the landing protocol?"

Rivka held her hands up. "Of course," she finally agreed. Sarcasm would be lost on the EI so she saved it, thinking of ways to improve her point and counterpoint with Grainger. "Let us know when we've docked. I have a list of people I need to interview, and I'd like to start those as soon as possible."

"You can contact them now if you would like."

Rivka looked at her notes. "Do that, please. I'll start with the governor, and we'll work our way backward."

"Communications channel is open," Chaz replied.

"Good morning, Magistrate. I'm Governor Flikansador, and I'm surprised that the Federation sent someone of your station to deal with this issue. *Pleasantly* surprised and quite honored, if I may say so."

Rivka heard the politician in his voice. She was afraid she'd sound young and he'd be patronizing, but she was the Magistrate and wielded authority that superseded his.

No matter how young she was.

"I'm not amused at being here, Governor. There are real crimes in this universe that warrant a Magistrate's attention, but what I see here is a family squabble wrapped in politics. No matter. I'm here, and I will deal with this. I'm forwarding a list. Bring each to an interrogation room sealed from all outside intrusion and keep them isolated until I call for them."

"Very well," the governor agreed softly. "I expect you'll keep us appraised while the process is ongoing."

"I will not. You will find out the adjudication at the same time as everyone else—when I make it public, and not before. When you called in the Federation to resolve your personal problems you handed all authority to us, and to me in particular. Magistrate Rivka out." She drew a line across her throat to close the channel.

"I can slap the shit out of him if he crosses you again," Red offered.

Rivka chuckled. "He sounded like a weasel. *I* could probably slap the snot out of him until he was begging for breast milk."

"I will watch your back. Men like him have people like me."

Rivka pursed her lips as she contemplated the wisdom of Vered's observation. "I am comfortable knowing that you have my back. I also see why Grainger hired you. You're a good man, Red. Thank you for taking the job."

The ship settled into a berthing slot and an extendable tube clamped to the airlock.

"Now, what do you say we go resolve this bullshit so we can go home?"

"Stay behind me, ma'am. You know the SOP."

"Which means that I won't see anything except your back."

"Probably better that way, ma'am. You will have enemies on this station before you say your first word. You will gain enemies as they spread lies of what you're doing, and whatever you decide, you will earn even more."

"Is there any way I can do this without creating so many new enemies?" Rivka was concerned. She hadn't thought about an army of people who wished her ill when all she wanted to do was adjudicate the crime and deal with the criminal. "I have more to weigh than just the criminal mischief. I thought I would, but I didn't think it would have such a broad impact. I'll chalk that up to my inexperience. Thank you for your insight, Red. It means a lot to me."

He unbuckled his belt and stood, then stretched before putting on his armored vest. He added a loose jacket on top of it to conceal the hardware he carried. He had demonstrated his abilities with firearms on the shooting range. Rivka could generally hit what she was aiming at, but he *always* hit it, and often in the bullseye. He shook off the accolades she had tried to give. *"It's different when they're shooting back. Way different,"* he'd said every time.

Rivka had excelled with improvised weapons, which gave her new confidence. Wherever she looked, she saw something that could help her survive if a situation went into the toilet.

Red led her off the ship, through the airlock, and onto the space station of the Intripas System. Red grunted and stepped aside.

Her eyes darted everywhere at once after she saw the small group before her. A man in front, clearly the governor. His wife to the side and one step back. On the other side and two steps back was a lackey. They stood in a corridor with no decorations; nothing to use in case of a fight. She appraised the three before her as Red looked down the corridors beyond. He wasn't concerned about the greeting party.

Rivka offered her hand. "I'm Magistrate Rivka," she said coolly.

"Governor Flikansador," the man replied, shaking her hand. He tried to give her hand a manly squeeze, but she squeezed back until he winced in pain before she let go. Neither of the other two offered to shake hands.

"I'm the governor's wife," the woman said.

"Surely you have a name," Rivka replied.

"Flutterby." The woman looked uncomfortable as she spoke her name.

Flutterby Flikansador. I guess I wouldn't tell people my name either, Rivka thought. "Flutterby is a beautiful name." Rivka smiled easily at the sad face. She'd seen too many women in the shadows of their men. Flutterby looked like she deserved better.

"I'm Superintendent Thidney," the other man said from behind the governor.

"If I had to guess, Thidney, I'd say you're my handler, ushering me wherever I need to go and reporting back to the governor at every turn. No, thank you. I'll find my own way." She tapped the datapad in her hand.

Governor Flikansador's face turned sour. "If you need anything, anything at all, please don't hesitate to ask." He turned with a flourish and strode briskly away, his wife and the superintendent hurrying to keep up.

Rivka wanted to say something smart, but Red was occupied by his job. She was probably being recorded, so maintaining her decorum took on new importance. "Chaz, show me the way," she ordered the datapad.

"I'm sorry, but I don't know the way," the EI responded. "The governor didn't share where the room was."

Swallowing her pride, Rivka took off running after the official and yelled, "Governor!" She slowed to a dignified walk before he turned. "On second thought, I may have been hasty. I would be honored to have the superintendent escort me."

The governor let a smirk creep into his expression

before he wiped it away. He snapped his fingers, and the superintendent nodded. The governor and his wife walked away arm in arm, at a much slower pace than before.

"Lead on, Super." Rivka motioned for the man to lead the way. He pointed behind her.

"Superintendent Thidney," he corrected as he brushed past. She clamped her mouth shut and glared at the back of his head as he took her through a maze of corridors. She had kept her datapad out and had run a live feed to Chaz the entire time. She didn't want to rely on the government of the space station any more than absolutely necessary.

She wanted to take a shower to wash away the station's stains.

He finally reached a corridor with chairs outside a single door. The people sitting next to each other watched the Magistrate approach. She tapped the superintendent on the shoulder. "You and I have a vastly different definition of the word 'sequester.'"

The man shrugged. Rivka didn't know what else to expect by way of an answer. "Stay out here and make sure they don't talk to each other. Red, stay with him and block the door. I'll be fine in there with whoever I'm talking to at the moment, although the first person on my list isn't here. Please have him report within the next ten minutes."

"The governor will not talk to you here!" the superintendent exclaimed.

"He sure as fuck will."

"Or what?"

"I leave and report his obstructionism to the Federation. Next thing you know, the station will be looking for a new governor. From what I've seen, I'm not so sure that would be a bad thing. Nine minutes and fifty seconds. I'll be inside."

Rivka went into the room. Cameras looked down on the table from each of the four corners. The Magistrate pulled a challenge coin, a coin with the logo of the Magistrates' Office, and threw it at one camera, shattering the lens. She recovered her coin and dispatched the other three cameras. She flipped the coin in the air, caught it, and slapped it onto her forearm. "Heads, you lose," she declared before returning it to her pocket.

She took a seat and accessed her datapad. Rivka looked at the screen but didn't see anything. Her mind was focused on the questions she needed to ask the governor. Her mind played and replayed numerous scenarios before Governor Flikansador walked in.

He wasn't alone.

"I brought my lawyer. I hope you don't mind."

"Not at all, as long as he doesn't speak. One word comes out of his mouth, I will throw him out of here and hold you in contempt. Please be seated."

Rivka sat on her side of the table, and the governor sat on his. There weren't any other chairs.

"When were you first made aware of the vandalism to the shops on the station?"

The governor looked at his lawyer, who nodded. "About a month ago. I'm sure you have the reports in your pad. They'll give the exact date."

"They give the date the report was made, but when were *you* made aware?"

"When the report was filed. I get a read-package each

morning, so it would have been the day after the report was filed."

Rivka tapped her screen. She wasn't writing anything down. She only wanted him to think she was. "When did you come to believe that the damage was caused by Jayita Flikansador?"

"Jay told us herself after we received the fifth or sixth report."

"And what did you do?"

The governor looked to the lawyer, who shook his head and held a finger to his lips.

"Under the advisement of my legal counsel, I won't be answering that question."

Rivka closed her eyes, counted to ten, and stood up. She walked slowly around the table to face the governor's lawyer. He puffed out his chest, and she smiled and delivered a punch that tagged him right on his twig and berries. The man collapsed. Demonstrating the strength of the nano-enhanced, she picked him up like a piece of luggage, lumbered to the door, opened it, and tossed him into the corridor. She closed the door softly behind herself, flipping the deadbolt before turning to find the governor standing. Rivka pointed to his chair and stabbed her finger at it until he sat.

She resumed her position in the interrogation, the position of Federation authority. "What did you do when your daughter told you she was responsible for the vandalism?"

"I grounded her," he whispered.

"Did you know for certain that she did it?"

"What?" He looked confused and started fumbling with

his fingers. "I never questioned it. I believed her. It seemed to fit."

"Did she *stay* grounded?"

"She's seventeen. What do you think?" Rivka rolled her finger. "No. She was out before we could finish dinner."

"Do you have any hard evidence that weighs against your daughter?"

"There's video."

"I need to see it."

"Lots and lots of video."

"Fine, transmit it to my ship. Chaz will examine the footage."

The governor pulled a pad from his pocket and tapped the commands. His shoulders slumped and he leaned heavily on the table, looking down.

"What did you expect when you summoned a Magistrate to deal with a misdemeanor?"

"Not this."

Too bad, Rivka thought. *This is what you got.* "I'm going to cut to the chase. Send Jayita in, please."

The man left without making eye contact or saying another word, leaving the door open. There was a scuffle in the corridor. Rivka leaned back in her chair and waited. A young woman with glowing pink hair walked in, looked at the table, and crossed her arms as she leaned against the wall.

"Close the door and take a seat, please," Rivka directed.

The young woman dialed up her middle finger and held it in front of her.

Rivka casually walked to the door, closed and bolted it, and turned to the young woman. "Just take a seat."

The woman held her middle finger in front of her as if it were a shield.

The Magistrate moved too quickly for the eye to follow. She grabbed the middle finger and leaned into it, and Pink Hair dropped to her knees. With a quick twist and pull Rivka dislocated the offending digit, then used it as leverage to drag the screaming woman to the table and dump her into the chair.

Rivka sat down on her side of the table and motioned for the woman to hold out her hand. The young woman looked furious, but the pain gave her pause. She winced as she stretched her hand out, and Rivka took it and popped the finger back into place.

During their brief contact, Rivka could feel the emotional turmoil within the woman, her trials, and her spirit. Rivka knew what she had to do.

"We need to have an understanding if this has any chance of getting resolved in all our best interests. I expect that I am now your father's mortal enemy, possibly your mother's, and also yours. I'm not a fan of being anyone's mortal enemy, so what do you say we get to the bottom of this, wrap it up, and we all go home? I expect that you are Jayita."

"Jay," the woman corrected softly while massaging her hand. "I did it. I did it all. I saw no other way to escape. That's all there is, so take me away."

10

"That's not how it works."

"I think it is. You're a Magistrate. You make the ruling, and you mete out Justice. You have the authority." Jay reached across the table and grabbed the Magistrate's wrist. "Save me!"

Rivka pulled her hand away and leaned back in her chair, steepling her fingers before her. "Prison sucks."

"How would you know?"

"I've been there. It sucks. I was accused of murder. I have a temper, you see, but it was in the course of Justice, so here I am, wondering why I'm here." Rivka leaned forward, resting her elbows on the table so she could look into Jay's eyes. "Why am I here, Jay? This is a free universe. Walk away. Leave. Join a freighter's crew. Take control of your life. Jail is just someone else telling you what to do, another place with no control."

"But they won't let me go!" she blurted.

Rivka accessed her datapad. Chaz had his report ready

from the videos. There was no doubt; the evidence showed that Jay had damaged the shops. That, combined with the confession, was enough to convict her, but the criminal mischief charge had been manipulated by the governor. The damage reports had been amended to lesser amounts. The insurance adjusters quoted much higher figures, high enough to turn a cry for help into a felony.

"You've put me in a bad position." Rivka stood. "Jayita Flikansador, I'm charging you with Felony Misconduct and Making Terroristic Threats. You will be temporarily incarcerated on my ship while I collect more information."

Jay hung her head. "Jhiordaan?"

Rivka clenched her jaw. "I haven't determined that yet."

The young woman looked relieved, but Rivka didn't know which part had caused it and she didn't ask. The Magistrate swept up her datapad and headed for the door, crooking a finger for Jay to follow. When she opened the door, the witnesses were still in the corridor, including the governor and his red-faced lawyer.

"I don't need to do in-person interviews. Thank you for your patience and understanding." Rivka addressed Red, who watched the people grumble as they shuffled away. "Take her to the ship and secure her in the holding cabin."

"No can do," Red replied as he glared at the governor.

"What's going on? What is the ruling?" the man asked.

"It's still in process. I am securing the prisoner until I can make a final determination," she replied to the governor before turning back to Red. "What do you mean, 'no can do?'"

"If I'm securing the prisoner, I can't guard you. My job

is to guard you, so it looks like all three of us are going to the ship."

Rivka appraised him before motioning for Jay to lead the way. With her head proudly in the air, the young woman marched down the corridor. Rivka followed the flowing pink hair, and Red fell in behind where he could watch in front as well as check behind them. The governor started to follow.

"Governor is following us," Red whispered.

"Governor?" Rivka yelled over her shoulder. "I will meet you and your wife in your quarters. Please send directions to my ship so I can get myself there."

Red pointed at the governor and shook his finger, making it clear that the man wasn't to follow. He stopped, and Red watched until they turned a corner. When they reached the next corner, Red declared them free of a tail.

"Listen, Jay. I don't have a cell on board my ship. I have an EI called Chaz who will answer any questions you may have. Make yourself at home, and by all that's holy, don't break anything."

"What does she want?" Flutterby demanded.

"I don't know. I don't know anything. This situation has spiraled out of control. I thought we'd have a nice dinner with the Magistrate and let him put the fear of God into Jay, then he'd leave. I never imagined they'd send someone who actually would try to do the job!"

The governor's wife started slapping his arm and shoulder. "You moron! You think you can control everyone, but you can't control jack shit. This was the worst gamble you've ever made. What's going to happen to me when you get removed from office?"

"What's going to happen to *us*, you mean? We'll move, start a new life elsewhere. We have friends," he told her dismissively.

"When you're not governor, you'll find that you have no friends. And I meant *me*, not us. I like this lifestyle, and if you have to die to keep providing it for me then you will," she replied coldly.

"Honestly, Flutter, I have no idea where this hostility is coming from." The governor used his most soothing voice.

"Don't project your political crap on me. You're such a dick." She stormed away, slamming the door to their bedroom. The governor looked at the closed door for a moment before pouring himself a drink.

"How to get out of this minor issue. Time heals all wounds, as they say, so with a few deft touches it'll be like the Magistrate was never here. Or maybe we could offer something of value. Can Magistrates be bought? Maybe not. I better not try that, but the witnesses? We already tried once. Maybe we can pay off all the damage. No, no, no," he argued with himself. "I'd have to take out a loan to do that. Let's see what she has to say. You've always been good on your feet. Show her what you're made of, but take care she doesn't knee you in the balls."

The governor chuckled at the memory of his lawyer's face when the Magistrate had tossed him into the hallway. *Simpering fool.*

"I'll have to play the High Chancellor card."

"Are you sure she'll be okay by herself? You could cuff her to the bed."

"I'm not sure, but I'm not cuffing her to the bed, either. I saw into her mind, Red. In the safety of the ship I think she'll find solace, a peace that she may never have had."

Red didn't argue. "Let me enter the ship first when we return to make sure she hasn't set any traps for you."

"Deal," Rivka replied.

They followed the map the governor had provided. His quarters were on the far side of the station, forcing the Magistrate to traverse it all on her way. She noted that there were ship berthing locations much closer to his quarters. *All part of the game,* she told herself.

They continued in silence, Rivka nodding pleasantly to the people she passed. She couldn't see the expression on Red's face, but most people moved out of the way of a large man walking with a purpose. He had a striking beauty that drew the eye of many, and Rivka smiled to herself as she watched. Red didn't show that he saw, but he had to notice.

The man seemed to see everything. The more he was around, the safer she felt. She reminded herself never to take that for granted. He would use his body to shield her if need be. Rivka wondered what he would accept as a bonus. She thought about an All Guns Blazing gift card, but when would he be able to use it?

She jerked herself back into the moment. The governor and his wife were waiting for her. When she demanded to see them, she didn't have a plan in mind. She only wanted to touch the woman and see what was in her mind. She still needed to ask questions to make it official.

When they arrived, they found two armed guards outside the entrance. One of them held up a hand. "You're armed," he declared, nodding toward Red's jacket.

"No shit," Red deadpanned. "Magistrate is here to see the governor, and she always travels with an armed guard. Announce the Magistrate and open the door."

"You can't enter the governor's presence armed."

"I've already been in the governor's presence armed. Why don't you guys travel with him around the station if there is such a threat to his life?"

"We do, but you don't see us."

"If I didn't see you, it's because you weren't there." Red pointed over his shoulder with his thumb. "The Magistrate is waiting."

"But you can't enter while you're armed."

"Who else is in there?" Red demanded, looming over the man.

"Just the governor and his wife." The man tried to push the bodyguard away, but he was too big.

"Good enough. I'll wait out here where you two can make me feel safer," Vered said. He winked at Rivka as he studied the corridor around them. The guard clicked the buzzer, and the door popped open. The guards stepped aside, and she walked through.

"Magistrate!" the governor called from across a large and lavish space. He put a drink down and hurried to offer his hand. "I hope we can start again on a new footing." He smiled broadly, showing a row of perfect teeth. "What news do you have of my daughter?"

"I'd like to talk with Flutterby, if I may."

As if summoned, a door opened and the governor's wife walked out, striding gracefully in a mid-length dress and heels as if she were headed for a cocktail party. The governor wolf-whistled and she stopped to take a bow.

Rivka stifled a gag and fought the urge to roll her eyes, deciding to smile instead. She needed to make physical contact if her gift was going to be of use. She walked forward and held her hand out, but the governor's wife brushed past her hand.

"We're huggers here," she declared before embracing Rivka. When their bare necks touched, the images started to flow. They were disparate and carried too much darkness to see clearly. The woman had a troubled soul, but was it driving her or she driving it? Rivka didn't have enough control over the visions to know. She wondered briefly if she would *ever* have control over her gift.

Flutterby suggested they sit on the overstuffed couch and matching chairs. *I wonder what it cost to bring those behemoths way out here,* Rivka thought as she picked a chair facing the station's First Couple. She settled in and smiled deeply. "This is nice," she commented graciously.

"We get by," the governor replied. Rivka ignored him.

"I have some disturbing information that I hoped you could shed some light on," she started. The governor and his wife looked at each other before turning their concerned faces toward the Magistrate. "Someone changed the official numbers in the police reports so the damage seemed less extensive. The insurance reports suggest the crime is felony misconduct, not the misdemeanor of criminal mischief."

Flutterby was shocked, but quickly regained control over her expression. The governor slowly adopted a look of surprise. "An overzealous aide, no doubt," he suggested smoothly, but sweat started to bead on his forehead. "I'm sure there is a middle ground somewhere that doesn't raise this to a capital crime."

"It's not a capital crime. No one will be executed for this."

"Whew, what a relief. We have a jail here on the station and will immediately incarcerate the prisoner. How long is the sentence?"

"I am still looking into extenuating circumstances."

"But surely you have enough already?" The governor struggled for words.

"What I have is an incomplete report. We all answer to someone, don't we, Governor? The High Chancellor will expect a thorough report, and I refuse to disappoint him."

"How is old Wyatt? We talk every week, my friend and I, but this week we'll have so much to talk about!" The governor smiled broadly. His wife assumed an artificial smile as she sat motionless.

Rivka didn't take the bait. "Jay was driven to those acts by you, wasn't she, Flutterby?"

The smile never cracked. "I'm sure I don't know what you mean."

The governor started to lose his carefully-manicured composure. "You did what?" he asked incredulously.

"I'm sure I don't know what you mean," Flutterby reiterated.

"I don't need you to answer. I already know."

No one spoke. The governor and his wife wondered if it was a bluff. So did Rivka.

"I should go. Thank you for your time," Rivka said abruptly.

"That's it? What's the adjudication?" the governor blurted.

"Oh, that!" Rivka assumed the thinker's pose as she tapped her lips with one finger. "She has already confessed to the act, which was felony misconduct, plus the videos showed her making terroristic threats, so two felonies, carry the one, subtract seven for time served already..." Rivka let it linger as she looked around the governor's quarters. "Nice place you have here. Too bad your daughter will spend the rest of her days on Jhiordaan."

Rivka's jacket swirled as she turned to head for the door.

"*Wait!*" the governor yelled in a voice laced with hysteria.

The Magistrate kept walking although she heard the slapping running feet behind her. When they got close, she dodged to the side and grabbed a lamp to use as a club. She crouched and prepared to fight. The governor and his wife pulled up short, their hands held in front of them with palms out.

Rivka put the lamp down. "What?"

"You can't commit her to Jhiordaan!"

"I most certainly can." Rivka's lip raised in a half-snarl.

Flutterby screamed and broke into tears, then flopped onto the floor and held her face in her hands as she started to sob.

"Whatever you did to her," Rivka pointed at Flutterby

and the governor, "her way of getting back at you was to destroy herself, the one person who should have brought you two closer together. Jay is coming with me, and I will personally mete out her Justice. Now, get out of my way. I have a report to write."

She elbowed the governor on her way past, throwing the door open and storming out. Red fell into step behind her without comment, his eyes constantly scanning the route and all access points to it.

11

Rivka tapped her foot impatiently as she waited for Red to verify that the ship wasn't boobytrapped. "It's clear, but you're not going to like it."

"What now?" she grumbled, walking to the bridge, then to the main room. The beginnings of a mural had been painted on the wall. She looked closer; figures were outlined for future work. "We had paint on board?"

"I had it delivered. I hope you don't mind," Jay said, holding a small palette and paintbrush.

"Chaz," Rivka called conversationally. "Please undock the ship and take us home."

"I'll wait in my room," Jay suggested.

"Why? You have a mural to finish."

The young woman perked up. "But what's going to happen to me after I finish?"

"I guess the mural of your life will never get to be finished then, will it? I have a report to write, and everyone is stopping me from doing it." Rivka strolled down the corridor and entered her cabin. After she closed the door, she went to her pull-out sink to splash water on her face. Her hand had a small tremor, something she'd never had before. "What the hell is going on with me? Damn nanocytes are making me weird."

She sat down on her bunk and looked at the plain metal walls. *You were weird before the nanos,* She admitted to herself.

Rivka remained in her cabin after the corvette passed through the Gate and returned to the station she thought of as Magistrate Central.

"Chaz, open a secure channel to Grainger."

Static crackled through the speaker. Etheric-powered devices didn't crackle like that. She assumed the EI was adding the sound so the humans knew he was doing what had been requested.

"You're back already?"

"Now who's asking the obvious questions?" she asked, sighing with relief at the familiar banter.

"Not really. That was a guess, since you could have called me from anywhere and you'd still sound the same. That Ted guy is a genius when it comes to this stuff. We have it all, thanks to him."

"I don't know that Ted guy, but I'll buy him a beer for making my life easier—assuming I'm still in a position to buy him a beer."

"That sounds ominous. What did you do?"

"I counted on my insight to find the real perp, and I punished her and her husband by telling them that their daughter was condemned to Jhiordaan when I simply added her to my ship's crew."

"I thought it was a misdemeanor?"

"And *I* thought Magistrates didn't deal with trivial crimes."

"Point taken. It was a felony." He made it sound like a question.

"The governor, I think it was him but didn't bother to gather evidence on it, cooked the books to make it look like a misdemeanor. Their daughter did a lot of damage to get back at her parents. There's nothing wrong with her. She just needed a change of environment and to get away from that toxic wasteland she called home."

Rivka could hear Grainger breathing, but he didn't reply.

"I guess I'm not cut out to be a Magistrate. My first case, and I wreak havoc on a Federation member's space station. I jacked his lawyer in the ghoulies."

"Lawyers are bastards! We should probably fire them all."

"Hey!" Rivka countered. "In any case, we'll be docking shortly. I'll turn in my jacket and submit myself for punishment for my original crime."

"Like bullshit, you will. If anyone has to apologize, it's me. I threw you into the middle of a domestic squabble at High Chancellor Wyatt's request. He knows that governor is a self-serving meathead."

"Plausible deniability? No matter what I did, it would show that the High Chancellor was doing something. He saves face, and if it went south, it was my fault."

"Something like that, but we had the utmost confidence in you. Sounds like you reached a solution that will work. I'll talk with the High Chancellor, but I expect he'll support your story. As for you, I look forward to your final report, but you will want to pick up fewer strays unless you want to buy a bigger ship out of your paycheck."

"I can afford a bigger ship?" she asked.

"No, you can't. Ha!" He laughed uproariously.

"I used to like you," she told him as she prepared to leave her cabin.

"I'm the funniest guy I know. Wait until I've had a few Supernovas and really get going!"

The ship settled into its berth, and the now-familiar clunk of the retractable access tube sounded throughout the corvette.

"Going ashore, Chaz," she declared.

"I'm sorry, but we are still in space."

Rivka walked down the corridor to where Red was waiting to lead her onto the space station. "Come on, Jay. Let me introduce you to the team, and we need to buy you some new clothes."

"I'm not going to jail?"

"Of course not. Why would I put a member of my crew in jail? And you'll probably need to change your hair color too, just in case prying eyes are looking for you."

"What if I don't *want* to go into the Pod-doc?" Rivka asked. Grainger shook his head and sighed.

"You have to, because," he replied as if that was explanation enough.

She stared at him, hands on hips, unmoving.

"A little bigger, a little stronger, and fix your shit so you don't have to go back to the dentist. There was a minor glitch in your previous nano load."

"You sent me into the cosmos with glitchy techno-bugs?"

He furrowed his brow and pursed his lips, then nodded once. "Yes, I did."

She looked back and forth to make sure no one was near enough to hear. "Are you making this shit up as you go? I'm not feeling the confidence."

"And now you know why those folks with titles that sounded like 'Grainger' were given such a rough reception."

"But the law..."

"The law doesn't change. Interpretations may vary, but the law is the law. It is the foundation on which we built this universe. What you did in Intripas reinforced that. No one is above the law. No one can interfere with getting to the bottom of an issue. And when it comes time for Justice, no one gets in our way."

"I thought Bethany Anne built this universe based on force of will and a vicious roundhouse."

"And we're here to keep it running smoothly when she's not around. The Queen counts on us."

"Fine." Rivka undressed and climbed into the Pod-doc, closing the door behind her. The technician started spinning things up.

"A porn queen's eyes?" Grainger whispered into the man's ear.

"Hey, don't sneak up on a guy like that." He scrubbed at his ear as if it had been tickled. "You wanted exotic and unique. Well, there's only one porn star with those eyes. Why do you know that?"

"I'm a Magistrate. We know everything."

"Your AI probably told you."

"A Magistrate never reveals his secrets," Grainger replied. "Add two more centimeters in height, improved hearing, and give her the full combat package."

"A full combat package? Have you been watching too many *RoboCop* reruns or something?"

"Sorry, she's not a cyborg, but imagine if she was!"

The technician waved at Grainger to go away. "It'll take about an hour," he called to the Magistrate's retreating form.

Red grunted as he hit the mat. That was three engagements in a row that Rivka had gotten the drop on him. "I like getting paid to work out, but I'm not good with getting paid to be a punching bag."

"Or get beaten up by a girl."

Rivka glared at Grainger.

"I didn't say it," Red replied, still lying on his back. "Magistrates are beating up on me. I see nothing else. Maybe I can get some Pod-doc time."

Grainger didn't say no.

"Maybe," Rivka suggested as she returned to the weights and powered through another set.

"Where's your crewman?" Grainger asked.

"This isn't for her," Rivka answered.

"She needs to be in shape."

"Jay is recovering. The solitude is her choice, plus, she's putting a nice touch of paint on the inside of the ship."

"Did you name it yet?"

Rivka shook her head and wrapped her hands quickly to prepare for another sparring round.

Red crouched, balanced on the balls of his feet with his hands raised. Grainger nudged him out of the way. "My turn."

Rivka shrugged, then dropped and spun trying to sweep the Magistrate's leg. He stomped on her leg, which stopped her cold, and danced backward to give her space to get up.

She stood, keeping her eyes fixed on her opponent. She waded toward him, feinting to draw his attack, but he didn't bite. He moved cautiously around the circle, working her impatience until she made an ill-advised attack. But she had learned a great deal in their matches, improving each day.

Rivka moved with him, remaining balanced and staying just out of reach.

Red made snoring noises and snapped his head as if waking up. "You guys are killing me. Get on with it while we're still young enough to enjoy our off-time."

The opponents continued to circle.

Grainger jumped forward, closing to within arm's reach. Rivka delivered a flurry of blows, most blocked by her opponent. She shouted when a random uppercut caught him on the chin, but her joy was short lived. He fell away from her to clear space for a back kick that sent her flying out of the sparring area into the weight machine.

Rivka rolled to her back. Red paced from the spot of

the kick to the machine. "Seven meters, give or take. That was a good one!"

The bodyguard headed for the shower, with Grainger close behind. No one helped Rivka to her feet. "Thanks for that," she grumbled and closed her eyes, willing her nanos to repair the bruise to her coccyx.

And ego.

"A meeting of Magistrates?" Rivka asked.

"Yes. There will be five of us. You'll get to meet a few of your peers, but there won't be time for socializing. We'll review new assignments, and by the end of the day I think all of us will be on our way out there to do our jobs and make the universe a safer place," Grainger replied. "Let's stop here first. I have something for you."

"I hope it's chocolate. This latest round of enhancements has given me a sweet tooth something fierce. I am shamelessly eating a pound of E&Es a day." She wondered if she should worry about her seeming addiction to the newest product from Knox Chocolates, but decided to worry about it later. She had more important things on her plate.

"It's not chocolate!" He shook his head as he pointed to a door and hurried that way.

"You made me this way with your damn techno-bugs."

"They're not mine. They're the Federation's bugs, and you better be nice to them."

"I'm not sure I can demonstrate any higher respect for them than by feeding them nearly endless supplies of chocolate. And Coke. I find that I like the sugar in the Coke. Are you buying me a Coke?"

"No Coke!" He stopped to give her a hairy eyeball. "Can you think about something other than your stomach?"

"Sure, but not right now. I'm hungry. It's been what…a good two hours since I last ate? Gotta keep the furnace stoked. That's what it's like when you run as hot as this little engine." She thrust one hip out and stuck her nose in the air.

"I should have sent you to Jhiordaan," Grainger muttered, grinning before motioning with his head to keep going. In the small storeroom, Grainger dug out a Magistrate's jacket. He snapped his fingers and she handed his back to him.

"Nice! And it's already a bit weathered." She held it up to herself before trying it on. She sniffed it, but couldn't place the smell. She turned left and right, admiring how she looked in the properly-fitting jacket. "Where'd this one come from?"

"That belonged to Magistrate Felcario Renaldo Squitieri. He died in the line of duty."

Rivka started to remove the jacket, but Grainger stopped her.

"What greater testament to what we do than to have the tools of our trade carry on? These jackets let everyone know who we are. Perps who challenge us will find themselves on a slab in the morgue or breaking rocks somewhere. If you don't make it, someone else will pick up the torch and keep going. What would the Federation be without the rule of law? Anarchy? Chaos? There would be no Coke, no Knox Chocolates, nothing being traded from one system to another if we didn't have a legal framework in which business could be conducted and in which decent people can live their lives free from the intrusion of others."

"I love the law," Rivka stated. "I like fair pay for fair work. I like it when people aren't afraid. We are their champions, standing between the lawless and civilized society."

"People shouldn't have to take up arms to protect themselves, so we do it for them. The only ones who should be afraid when they see this jacket are the criminals."

"Especially when those criminals are the ones who are supposed to enforce the law." In her memories, Rivka saw the governor and his wife sitting on their overstuffed couch in their decadent quarters as they tried to manipulate the law to their advantage. "Fuck those guys."

Grainger nodded. "Indeed. And now we have a meeting to get to."

12

"They call me 'Cheese Blintz,'" a short man told her, flashing a broad grin. He laughed at Rivka's curious expression. "Chi Siblinz is my real name, but these Neanderthals can't seem to get that right."

She leaned close. "Embrace the chi," she told him, and winked.

"I like you already!" He made way for the other two in the plush meeting room.

"I am Jael," a woman said in a deep voice. They shook hands.

"I'm Rivka. Rivka Anoa."

"Rivka Rivka Anoa is a bit of a mouthful, but if that's how your tribe names its kids, who am I to argue?"

"No, it's just Rivka," she replied, confused.

"Well, which is it? 'Just Rivka,' or 'Rivka Rivka Anoa?'" the woman pressed.

"Neither!"

"Now we're getting somewhere. Meet Nether, our

newest Magistrate!" the woman declared, stepping aside and motioning for Rivka to step forward.

"Now you see why I'm Cheese Blintz. He should have warned you." Chi pointed at Grainger, who looked over his shoulder to see who Chi was pointing at.

The man offered his hand. "They call me Bustamove." He was the same size as Grainger, with blond hair and piercing blue eyes. A thin scar showed white around the top of his head. He caught Rivka staring at it. "Almost lost my head in one of these meetings. They can be *so* boring."

"Sorry," Rivka mumbled quickly. "What's your real name? I am *not* calling you 'Bustamove.'"

"Buster Crabbe. My parents named me after some ancient movie star, or so I've been told. And the scar? Don't mess with the trilobites. They'll cut you."

"But trilobites are tiny sea creatures..." Rivka started, and the other four laughed. She instinctively looked for Red, but he was in the corridor. It struck her that no one else had a bodyguard. "Why am I the only one to have a bodyguard?"

"You're under the new budget. We're old budget, so we have to get along without. You can thank me for getting it included," Grainger told her smugly.

"Let's all get in line to kiss your ass," Jael said. "*Liebchen.*"

"Liebchen? Is that your real name?" Rivka wondered.

"Lieblen Schlongheim is my real name," he admitted, enunciating slowly, "but that can never leave this room."

"You gotta be shitting me." Rivka looked from face to face.

Grainger shrugged and pulled out the chair at the end of the table. The others took their seats. Rivka sat in the last empty spot. They put their datapads on the table and started to tap commands.

Rivka kept her hands in her lap. Grainger stopped, turned to her, tapped something on his screen, and pointed to her datapad.

"Access Granted to Rivka Anoa: Magistrate Case Files."

She touched the icon, and a full library appeared. She was fascinated by the sheer volume of information that was available. Even in law school, she hadn't had access to an entire universe's legal proceedings, precedents, and laws. She reached out a finger to start browsing when an icon popped up, turned red, and started spinning. Her only choice was to select that one.

She found Grainger smiling at her.

"I've put five files in the pending case directory. Take a quick look and then let's discuss."

The Magistrates started reading. Lawyers, doing what they did best; reading, assessing, fitting the actions within the legal framework, and seeing where they stepped outside of it. Some were easier to reconcile than others.

"Who's up for a serial killer?" Grainger asked.

"Torah 7," Jael replied. "I haven't had a capital case in a while, and this culture is different. Look at how the law is written. It's legal to kill people as long as the killer meets certain conditions under the law. Homicides, the killing of one person by another, are a daily occurrence, but murders, an illegal killing, are rare. And here we have a bunch of them. I think it'll be a nice getaway."

A nice getaway. Rivka picked her jaw up off the table.

"It's all you, Jael," Grainger agreed. She gave him the thumbs-up and stood.

"Time to get to it, then. I'll see you on the flip side, Liebchen. Nice to meet you, Nethers."

"Hey," Rivka replied weakly, returning the thumbs-up. The Magistrate left the room.

"And then there were four," Grainger said ominously.

"Schlongheim?" Rivka wondered.

Grainger rolled his eyes and looked at the next case. "We have an R2D2 research facility that the brass thinks has been penetrated, but they expect it's an inside job. Someone needs to go play computer forensics until you find the meat sack behind it."

"Ooh, me! Pick me," Buster exclaimed, throwing his hand in the air. *"Pick me!"*

"Why do *you* want it? You hate computers."

"My EI has ascended. Philko is now fully intelligent, so he'll do the heavy lifting. I want to see what kind of toys they're working on, maybe get myself the newest model of a Jean Dukes Special pistol. You know they go to eleven."

"I know. Philko, huh? Is he up for it?"

"Couldn't be upper," Buster replied.

"Bustamove it is. Wait one." Grainger tapped and swiped furiously. "Your clearances have been transferred. Upon arrival, you'll be given unrestricted access to everything in R2D2. Philko has the coordinates of the facility since they aren't near a Gate, so you can jump right next to them."

Buster waved to everyone while whistling an unsavory bar tune. He left without a word.

"I've heard of this crap," Grainger started, making a face. The case file on the screen simply said Blood Trade. "It's a holdover from Earth, the Blood Trade. Michael,

Terry Henry Walton, and Valerie all fought against it, but it seems to have made its way out here. Entrepreneurs are kidnapping anyone who is enhanced—the more enhanced they are, the better it is—and then the scumbags are draining their blood to sell on the black market. Drinking enhanced blood boosts life and strength without having to go through a Pod-doc.

"These are rich people who don't want to go to the Pod-doc or can't because they are criminals. They get some of the benefits without any of the exposure. Once they start drinking the blood, they can't stop. It's addicting, so it becomes a drug crisis on top of the vileness of it all. Blood addicts are the worst sort—complete disdain for anyone else.

"I'm going to claim executive privilege and go after these bastards. Looks like the planet Yoll for me, the seat of the Queen's empire. I'll hire some Yollin toughs to accompany me..." Grainger tapped the interface to request the funds and contacts. Having only glanced at the case, he already assumed the Yollins were behind it. He hoped to find facts to the contrary, but wasn't confident that he'd be proven wrong. He had a nose for these things.

"Next up is a cozy murder mystery on Shaiboloa. The reason they've asked for our help is that it's within the ruling circle. Ten of them went on a leadership retreat, but only nine returned. The location was secure, so it suggests one of the inner circle is the murderer."

"That sounds interesting," Rivka remarked.

"Mine," Chi blurted.

"You know the rules. First to claim it gets it."

"What rules? I don't know the rules. How about 'ladies first?'" Rivka wondered.

The two men started to laugh and high-fived each other. "Now you do. Congratulations Cheese Blintz, you're going sleuthing on an island getaway. Better go. They're in a hurry."

"Nice." Rivka pouted as she looked at the last file. "You suck."

"Gotta go, Nethers. See you when we get back. Since the Shlongmeister won't tell you the rules, here's another one you need to know. After one of these, first back buys the first round, to be reimbursed by the last one back. The best story gets to pick first next time. Capital crimes buy shots. And there're a few more. I'll shoot you a list before I Gate out of here." Chi shook Rivka's hand, gave Grainger the finger and walked out.

Grainger pointed to his datapad. "Let's see what the universe has in store for you."

Rivka started reading the file. "You have *got* to be shitting me."

"It's a trade dispute that could escalate into a war between neighboring planets. That is a big deal. We would usually send a more experienced Magistrate, but that's not what this one needs. Pretarians and the Keome are aliens who have a common ancestor, but they've both developed on their own worlds. Both are hotter climates than humans are used to. Part of your last upgrade in the Pod-doc will help you deal with that. Pretaria is an arid planet, desert-like, while Keome is rocky. You'd think they'd get along famously, but they don't. This accord is their first attempt, and it has gone off the rails in a big way.

"Magistrates to the rescue as part of the Federation arbitration commitment. We do it, not the usual toadies and lawyers, in case there is any subterfuge. As Federation signatories they are both obligated to comply, and should we find one of the governments conducting illegal activities to contravene the agreement, we can mete out immediate punishment. We are in a unique position to stop governments from playing that game. They all try it, but we make sure they don't get away with it. Punish the individual and let the government save face before they return to the negotiating table. On a personal note, I'm curious how your gift will work with aliens other than Yollins. These folks are both very tall and very alien.

"All righty, then! I'll see you when you get back. Good luck, fair winds, and peace, fellow human."

Rivka opened her mouth as if to ask a question but Grainger swirled past, slapping her hard on the shoulder, and was gone.

Red entered the room to make sure that Rivka was okay. He shrugged and headed back into the corridor, closing the door quietly behind him.

"All righty, then," Rivka repeated. "What the hell does that mean? What if my gift doesn't work, motherfucker? I get a sore neck from looking up at angry aliens? That sounds cool. Trade dispute, could lead to war. Very alien. Good luck. Let me get a big bucket and fill it with hopes and wishes and see how long that will last us," Rivka told the empty room. She cradled her head in her hands for a moment.

"All righty, then," she repeated with as much sarcasm as she could muster.

Rivka scrolled through the case file quickly, instantly memorized the salient points of law from both Pretaria and Keome, and left the room. "Come on, Red, we're going to stuff our faces with real chow before we have to eat that garbage on our ship."

"I *like* the ship's food," Vered replied as he headed toward Rivka's favorite restaurant.

The EI moved the ship away from the docking port and flew it into space.

"Chaz, take us out of the main shipping lanes and hold station," Rivka requested.

"Of course. May I ask why?"

"You can always ask, but I may not always answer, so please don't take offense."

"I can't take offense. I don't have emotions as you understand them."

"I want to finalize some things with my crew before we Gate to Pretaria. You are so efficient that once we start the process, we'll be there in fifteen minutes. I'm not ready to be there that quickly, so let's hold up until we are."

"Thank you, Magistrate."

Rivka looked at the speaker from which Chaz projected his voice and shook her head. *EI, my ass. He is as smart and as sentient as I am. I'll play along, though. I wonder if EIs get lower pay than AIs?*

"All hands on deck!" Rivka called. Red had checked the ship thoroughly to ensure there were no stowaways, as well as no traps. He kept a wary eye on Jay.

Red cradled his hand oddly, and Rivka nodded toward it. He uncovered it to reveal three parallel razor-thin lines from which blood seeped.

"What happened to you?"

"I fucking hate cats."

"It looks like Hamlet doesn't like you much, either."

"You leave him alone!" Jay called as she put the finishing touches on a character in her mural.

"That's taking shape nicely, Jay. What do you call it?"

"I call it the 'doesn't-have-a-name mural,'" she replied, setting her palette aside and heading for the sink to wash out her brush. "Until it does."

Rivka sat in one of the recliners, which conformed to her body automatically. She sighed. "I could get used to this."

Red was running the food dispenser. "You just ate!" Rivka exclaimed.

"I don't eat like I want to when I'm on the clock, no matter how much you tell me to." He studied the food as microwaves heated it. Jay glanced furtively in his direction before making a face at the concoction getting nuked.

"Fair enough." Rivka accessed her datapad. "We are going to arbitrate a trade dispute. No kidding, that's what we got for a job, but as with all jobs, we're going to do the very best we can to be fair to all parties within the confines of the law. These two worlds are on the brink of war, which would be disastrous to both. The Federation likes having access to their space, so a war would put a crimp in Federation trade. They want this resolved peacefully, but they weren't willing to commit the Force de Guerre or the Bad Company. I guess Magistrates come cheap."

Rivka continued to scroll through the case file, then transferred part of the data to the mess deck's viewscreen.

"Here is a graphic of the two worlds. They are in an identical orbit, but separated one-hundred and eighty degrees. They are both hot and dry, being equidistant from the same sun. The people are descended from a common ancestor, but those on each planet have evolved some unique traits. They are all seven to nine feet tall. The Pretarians have leathery orange skin with kidney-shaped yellow eyes. The Keome are tall with chameleon-like skin, but they developed multiple long arms and have eyes on both sides of their heads." She flashed pictures of both races on the screen.

"What are those?" Jay asked, pointing at the neck of a Pretarian.

"They have a penchant for wearing a lot of clacking beads," Rivka read. "That's what it says right here. Clacking beads. That'll be interesting."

Red watched with mild disinterest as he shoveled his food into his mouth.

"For you, Red, it looks like there may be some subterfuge between the parties. I think in these kinds of negotiations, there always is. I have no idea what or who. We're going to have to root that out. Each group is allowed to bring five people into the arbitration. Our translation chips have their languages uploaded, so our interaction with them should be seamless."

"I'll stay closer to you than usual until we find out what kinds of attacks are possible."

"'Possible' is a pretty broad range," Rivka suggested.

"That's what I got to work with," Red countered,

pointing to a note at the bottom of the screen. "Says Keome and Pretarian foods are toxic to humans. Your nanos will help if you ingest it, but it'll put you into a world of hurt. I insist you don't eat or drink anything they offer."

"That goes for all of us," Rivka agreed.

Jay finished cleaning her brush. "All of us?" She twisted her mouth back and forth. "I'm going with you?"

"Yes. Watch what there is to watch. I need someone to bounce ideas off. Between you and Red, I think we'll be able to work through this."

"Who is going to take care of Hamlet while we're gone?"

"We'll return to the ship to eat and rest, so I think that answer is 'all of us,'" Rivka told the girl.

"Not me," Red replied definitively through a mouthful of something unidentifiable.

"You said you hate dogs, too." Rivka looked up from her pad.

"Yep. Dogs, too."

"You know that the other Magistrates are werewolves?"

"I knew there was something off with that bunch," Red declared, getting up to return his dish to the food unit for recycling.

"You did not!" Rivka laughed. "And it doesn't matter. We each have our secrets and special skills. It's what makes us who we are. Chaz, prepare to Gate. We have two worlds to save."

13

Pretaria, looking brown and uninviting, filled the main screen.

"It's amazing that life evolved in such a place." Rivka rubbed her chin and clutched her datapad tightly. She wondered how long it would take her to feel confident when starting a new case. "Do you have clearance to land yet?"

"Not yet, Magistrate. No one is answering my request."

"I'd say keep at it, but you already know that. I'll be in my lounger. That's right, all of you heard it. I'm claiming that chair as inviolably mine."

"Inviolably?" Red wondered

"Means 'don't touch it.'"

"I figured as much." Red never took his eyes from the planet's image. Rivka could see the wheels turning—what kind of threats come from a desert planet or a chameleon-like race of multi-armed creatures? "How many aliens will be in the negotiations, and who is in charge of the site's security?"

Rivka shrugged. "I don't know. We'll have to ask. You may need to coordinate with their security."

"I'll do that before we touch down," Red replied and walked briskly away, calling back over his shoulder, "I'll be on the bridge."

Rivka stayed in her recliner and reviewed the information on the monitor, scrolling through screens of Federation law regarding arbitration.

Jay cleared her throat. When Rivka blinked and looked up from the screen, she found Jayita staring at her from a turned-around chair.

"That looks like the most boring shit I could imagine."

"It's the law: the ins and outs of the process, pitfalls to avoid, and points to keep before all parties. It's the roadmap to civilized society."

"So you say," Jay countered. Rivka didn't want to argue. Jay wasn't that much younger, but they were worlds apart when it came to experience with the universe. "They aren't going to play nice."

"What do you mean?" Rivka leaned forward, put her elbows on her knees, and held her face as she fixed her eyes on the young woman.

"Everybody wants something, and all of them are willing to lie to get it. When you understand what they want, you'll be able to shape your lies to counter theirs."

"Is that how you think?"

"Everybody lies," Jay affirmed softly.

"To some extent, yes," Rivka agreed. She kept her focus on Jay. "What are you proposing?"

"Nothing. Just keep your eyes open. Assume the words are lies, but watch what the body does. It can't lie—unless the aliens don't act like humans, but I've never seen that. Everyone, human and alien alike, gives their shit away."

"You are thinking of something. Do you want to be my eyes? Watch the aliens for tells and let me know when they aren't being completely truthful? I can pin them down. What good is my authority if I don't use it?"

Rivka didn't want to pull rank or flash the badge or do any of the variety of things that would declare superiority without actions that had earned respect.

Jay shrugged.

"You'll be with me, but try not to yawn."

"Trapped in a conference room with two groups of angry aliens arguing over a document. That sounds like a great time!" The sarcasm was heavy.

Rivka took a deep breath. "The paper is simply a vehicle by which they can vent and fume. It keeps them from attacking each other. If it breaks down into a fight, get behind me. We'll let them duke it out until we can seize control of the situation. I hope it doesn't devolve into that."

The Magistrate shook her head. The only thing she could think about was an alien scrum instead of the arbitration that was supposed to happen. Or maybe a hockey match would break out. She wasn't sure which, but if that was what happened, the other Magistrates would change her name from "Nethers" to "Brawling Betty."

"I have the security detail on track. We're heading to the landing coordinates now, Magistrate," Red yelled from the bridge.

"There *is* an intercom," she replied.

Rivka didn't argue with Red when he led the way from the ship. As soon as the hatch popped, a wave of heat boiled through it. The big man leaned into it as if walking into a hurricane, but there was no wind, only the intense heat.

"Buck up," she told Jay. The young woman gritted her teeth and nodded tersely. Red motioned, and they walked out side by side. Rivka's golden-blue hazel eyes adjusted instantly to the near-blinding light and her pupils contracted to pinpoints. Jay shaded her eyes with a hand. She blinked quickly and squinted against the brightness, even after her hand blocked most of it.

A small delegation of Pretarians was waiting for them. Using her peripheral vision, she took in her surroundings. A small landing field with three total ships. Three were spaceworthy: hers, the Keome vessel, and the intra-atmospheric transport belonging to the Pretarians.

Rivka thought she was prepared to meet creatures that were seven feet tall, but every member of the delegation was at the high end of the scale at nine feet, and they wore platform boots as well, making them even taller.

"Everyone lies," Jay whispered craning her neck at the Pretarian delegation.

"I bet the Keome sent their tallest as well."

Jay nodded. "Couldn't be outdone by those stubby Pretarians."

Red finally stepped aside to allow the women to pass and a new blast of hot air hit them in the face. Jay gasped, but Rivka kept her features neutral as she struggled against the heat, her nanocytes kicking into high gear to help her compensate. Neither Red nor Jay had that crutch to lean on.

Rivka tipped her head slightly in the way of a Pretarian greeting. Each in turn did the same, nodding their heads by swinging their necks, their beads clicking and clacking. The sounds were unique to each individual. Rivka wondered briefly if she would have been able to pick up the differences had her hearing not been enhanced, then accepted what was.

"That was a beautiful greeting. Thank you for sharing the sound of your art." Rivka nodded once again. The Pretarians repeated their ritual. They didn't offer a hand since shaking was a human custom, but Rivka needed to touch them.

"We humbly welcome you to Pretaria, the lead planet in the Pretarian system," the tallest and widest of the reception committee said. "I am Delegate Maseer, and this is the team Pretaria has entrusted with these most delicate and critical negotiations."

"The human custom is to shake hands to greet each other, and we do it when we make agreements, too. It keeps us grounded." She thrust her hand out and Maseer looked at it, then at his fellows.

"We'll work on that," Rivka offered after it became uncomfortable. She smiled and made to slap him on the shoulder, but it was out of her reach.

"Meet Rhonali, Tinashi, Ngobo, and Sinraloo." Maseer pointed as he said their names.

One by one she nodded as she walked down the line. The last one, Sinraloo, held out his hand. Rivka hurriedly took it, smiling at the Pretarian as she did, despite the alien thoughts that washed over her. Just like the planet, Sinraloo's mind was awash in browns and despair. His abject hatred of the Keome blazed vividly at the front of all his thoughts.

Rivka let go. "Shall we?" she asked as she forced herself to look away from the angry one.

Maseer led the way toward a nearby structure.

"I hope they have air conditioning," Jay whispered.

"I wouldn't count on it," Rivka muttered in response. Red closed in behind them, and Rivka turned back to find him sweating profusely and turning pale. "Are you okay?"

"Fine," he rasped, not sounding fine.

Rivka glanced back and forth between him and the building, which didn't seem to get closer as they approached. Red started to stagger, and she leaned back into him just as his eyes rolled back in his head. She stumbled beneath his weight but balanced him until she could let him fall over her shoulder. She hefted him in the fireman's carry. Jay was starting to sweat.

"If we could hurry," Rivka called as the delegation moved ahead. Maseer picked up his pace without looking back. The long legs of the Pretarians helped them to move quickly, and Rivka found herself running to catch up. Jay jogged alongside, her breathing getting more ragged with each step.

They entered the building to find that the temperatures weren't much different, but they were protected from the pounding of the sun.

"Humans appear to be ill-suited to our climate. Maybe the Federation can send one of its more robust species?" Maseer suggested.

Rivka ignored him as she forced Red to drink all the water he and she carried. Jay drank all that she had.

"If you would be so kind as to turn the temperature down a few degrees, we'll be fine. We would appreciate extra water as well, and would like to meet the Keome contingent as soon as possible."

At the mention of the Keome, the Pretarian delegation hissed and stamped their feet.

"We will call for water, but can't be sure when it will arrive," Maseer told her.

Rivka stood as tall as she was able and still had to lean back to see the Pretarian, like a child looking at her parent. "According to the Federation Rules of Arbitration, when an arbitration is requested, the host is required to provide appropriate physical accommodations. You were made aware of our needs. Failure to provide means that I will be required to rule in default of the other party. If I don't have water in here in five minutes, the Keome delegation will be awarded primacy. Period. A Magistrate's ruling in this arbitration would be final. Is that clear?"

Maseer didn't answer.

Everyone lies. The words came back to Rivka. *But this isn't a bluff, you goony bastard.*

She kept her name-calling to herself, given the dignity of the Magistrate's position, the authority, and the representation. The Rangers-turned Magistrates might seem to take a devil-may-care attitude toward their work, but she had been a barrister first, and that was still how she thought of herself.

She pulled her datapad from a pocket inside her jacket, which she had insisted on wearing despite the heat. "Chaz, move the ship closer to the building. It looks like we'll be leaving early."

"You cannot park the ship close to the building. It is forbidden," Sinraloo interjected. Maseer held up a hand.

"There is no need to move your ship. I have been informed that water is on its way and will be here momentarily. There was a miscommunication with our support staff, which will be corrected."

"Chaz, move the ship, please." Rivka glared upward at the Pretarian, and he waved urgently at the others. Sinraloo crossed his arms and stamped a foot. Rhonali hurried away, going through a door leading into the building from the main reception area. She returned shortly carrying a tray with three small glasses half-filled with a murky liquid.

Rivka clenched her fists and started to shake with the fury that threatened to take over her being. She closed her eyes and tried to think.

The rules of arbitration. Pretarian law. Everyone lies. Pretarian law. Water was sacred and not to be wasted. Rules of arbitration.

She opened her eyes and took one of the offered glasses. "I thank you very much for sparing this much of your planet's sacred resource for us mere visitors. We will move our ship close to supplement our needs. We require far more water than Pretarians."

Rivka saluted with her glass and drank it slowly. It tasted like mud, but she powered through it. "Jay, once the ship moves, if you would be so kind as to bring a jug or three I would greatly appreciate it. Then we can start what we came here for."

Jay wiped her brow. "It's a little hot in here," she stated, and started to laugh.

"Yeah, just a little."

"Fuck," Red exclaimed succinctly.

"*There* you are, sunshine. Are you okay? Do you need to go back to the ship to cool down?"

Red's skin was flushed, and he looked angry. Actually, he looked a mess. "I've gotten heat exhaustion one too many times, and now when I start getting hot, my body shuts down. I'm sorry. How did I get in here?" Red looked at the impatient Pretarian delegation.

Jay pointed to Rivka. "She carried your big ass."

"Fuck!" he reiterated. Rivka shook her head.

"Language," she cautioned with a wink. "We'll have a great deal more water shortly. When we get back, I'll recommend that you get Pod-doc time. Can't have me using your body as a shield again." She motioned for him and Jay to take the two other glasses of water, and they drank, grimacing.

The ship landed, and Jay went to the door. She took a deep breath as if preparing to dive into a pool and ran out. She lumbered back shortly with a five-gallon jug of water. She also had a bag.

She put the jug on the floor, and from her bag she removed five glasses and set them on the tray. Using a small pump attached to the top of the jug, she half-filled the five glasses and offered them to the Pretarians. She filled the three glasses from before and shared them with the humans.

Rivka smiled broadly. "Well done." She turned to the Pretarians. "Here is to a successful arbitration. May we leave with our dignity intact and an arrangement that is mutually beneficial."

The Pretarians critically looked at the liquid in their glasses, and Maseer signaled to the others that it was okay. He drank his first, and the rest of his delegation followed.

"Thank you. That was very good. Maybe we can talk separately about bringing water to our planet."

"Once the arbitration is complete, we will be more than happy to talk about that and other potential goods or processes for expanded trade with the Federation. Do you know that there are entire planets of nothing but water?"

Maseer didn't respond in a way Rivka understood. She studied his body language, but couldn't tell if his answer was yes or no.

The language outside the words would be critical to finding a resolution to the dispute with Keome. If the anger that Sinraloo had exhibited was representative of what the entire delegation felt, she didn't have high hopes.

I won't fail! she declared, steeling herself.

"The Keome are waiting in the negotiation chambers," Rhonali stated.

"When did they arrive?" Rivka wondered.

"They've been there this whole time."

That's how it's going to be, huh? "I think it best we not keep them waiting any longer. Red?"

"I'm fine," he assured her and stood up. Jay wrapped an arm around his waist to steady him. She searched for a place to hang on that wasn't lumpy from the weapons concealed beneath his vest. He tensed as he leaned against her. He wasn't one for such a public display of weakness.

Rivka walked to the door Rhonali had gone through earlier. "Shall we?"

Maseer led the way and Jay and Red forced their way forward to walk behind Rivka. The Pretarians shuffled their feet. Rivka now recognized it as their way of showing dismay.

When they reached the doorway, which was secured by two armed Pretarian guards, Rivka touched Maseer's arm to hold him back. His emotions rushed against her before disappearing as she stepped aside. He wasn't angry like Sinraloo. He was disappointed, and carrying a bone-deep sadness that he didn't share. His persona was gruff and hard. The sadness weighed on him.

He looked at the spot on his arm that Rivka had touched.

This is going to be more difficult than I thought. "Maseer, I know that your people are angry with the Keome. I'm sure they are angry with you too, for whatever the reason. But I am asking if you would look at this through fresh eyes. See it as I see it. Let reason guide you in the way that is best for your people."

He pointed to the door. "See for yourself before asking me to see as you do."

She contemplated his words for a moment before nodding and motioning toward the door.

"I'll wait out here with my two newest friends," Red told Rivka, freeing himself from Jay's grip to lean against the wall. It was cooler in this area, at least tolerable considering there was a jug of water to drink.

"Where's the bathroom?" Rivka asked as she looked at the jug of water.

Maseer pointed to a door behind Red. "And there's one in the conference room too, but we won't use that once the Keome have. I hope you understand."

"I don't, Maseer. I don't understand at all, but that's what we're here for. I think it's time."

Maseer took a deep breath and opened the door, jumping back immediately. Rivka looked inside. Five Keome jumped up from their seats at the table and started to yell. One rushed toward the door, waving his multiple arms. Rivka stepped in his way, but he kept coming. She braced herself and struck with all the strength her enhanced body could muster.

Her forward punch hit the Keome mid-stride, throwing him back into the two who followed. They caught him, and that stopped the momentum of the three.

"STOP!" she roared. She straightened her jacket and began anew in a more controlled tone. "I am Magistrate Rivka Anoa. I'm here to arbitrate your dispute. Physically attacking a Magistrate is a crime in the Federation, for which I can mete out punishment. Is that what you want? To be embarrassed in front of the Pretarians? You will conduct yourselves as official representatives of your respective planets, not iron-age barbarians."

"Why did you make us wait? We should have been allowed to greet the Magistrate outside in the fresh air and not in this ice cave," the only Keome who was still seated asked.

"Read the law. It's the host's responsibility, not yours. You have no say in this." Maseer stretched himself taller to loom over the Keome.

The representative finally stood. He was nearly as tall as

Maseer, but the four arms made him appear more imposing. As he turned, the eyes on the back of his head came into focus. Rivka found the four eyes far more disconcerting than the extra limbs. For reasons only evolution knew, the Keome had developed differently from the ancestor they shared in common with the Pretarians.

"We have an equal say, as parties to this negotiation and treaty."

"As of right now, we start fresh. Anyone who brings up something from the past that had no resolution will be docked against the final arbitration. Is that understood? Please introduce me to your delegation so we can get started."

"I am Yus, Primary for Keome. My second is Miento. Suarpok provides spiritual counsel, and Ome and Yutta are the Commoner representatives."

"Yutta, I trust I didn't hurt you too badly. Control yourself, and I will forget about your assault and battery. Please, everyone, take your seats. I'll need a second chair for Jay, and have a chair delivered for my bodyguard in the corridor."

The lone female Keome bowed and slid her chair toward the end of the table. She stood behind the others of her delegation.

"Thank you, Ome. That is very kind." Rivka looked at the chair, whose seat was even with her belly button. Jay made eyes at her before climbing into the chair, where her legs dangled a long way from the floor. Rivka climbed into her chair and fought the sensation of feeling like a little kid.

14

Rivka instantly hated the room arrangement. The Pretarians were directly across from the Keome, allowing the two sides to glare at each other, while she was at the end of the table with only her shoulders and up visible. It was like a kid sitting at the adults' table during Thanksgiving. She leaned back in her chair.

"We need a different venue. A round table that will seat twelve, please." She turned to Maseer.

"My apologies, Magistrate," he started, "but we do not have such a table. I am not trying to stall the negotiations." Rivka smiled at his defensiveness. She'd made him take more care in his attempt to manipulate her and the arbitration.

Jay shrugged. "Then we will all stand," she declared. "Help me turn this table on its side and move it against the wall."

The members of both delegations slid their chairs away from the table as Rivka stood and signaled which way to turn it. Maseer held out a hand to stop the efforts, but it was too late. The Keome were more than enthusiastic in dumping the Pretarian table on its side. They pushed it at the Pretarians, who jumped from its path.

"Enough!" Rivka yelled to get everyone's attention. "Here's the new arrangement." She walked from body to body and pointed where she wanted them to stand. She positioned two chairs between the ends of the arcs. Both groups now faced her more than each other.

Jay nodded in approval, staying to the left and half a step behind Rivka.

"Isn't this better?" Rivka asked, not waiting for an answer. "This is how we will be arranged for the remainder of the arbitration. Let me go over the ground rules. You will not bring up anything from the past that can't be resolved in the present. You will not call names. You will not resort to violence of any sort. And most importantly, you will listen when I speak."

She didn't bother to get an affirmation of the ground rules because the full rules were in the Federation's Law of Arbitration, to which both planets were signatories. She was being concise. She didn't want to beat them over the head with the rules; she wanted the rules to provide a framework within which the parties could negotiate in good faith.

Rivka opened her datapad. There were forty-seven contended points out of a grand total of forty-eight.

"Let's start with the single point not in contention," she began with a smile. Her smile disappeared as she read the sentence. "The planets that are bound by this treaty are called Pretaria and Keome."

"The fact that you could agree on that point, although it may seem ridiculous, is a start. From that foundation, a house shall be built. Moving to point two."

She looked up before continuing. Both groups stood still as statues. She glanced at Jay, whose eyes darted around the room as she looked for patterns from the aliens' body movements, but they were giving nothing away. She shook her head just enough to let Rivka know she hadn't found anything.

Rivka started to read. "The party of the first part shall receive the first Federation shipment, from which the following shipments shall alternate on a schedule aligned with Ingranalla's Tide, highest which, thereunto..." Rivka stopped. "This could be the absolute worst sentence I've ever read in my entire life."

"We are the party of the first part," Maseer informed her.

"You cannot be. Keome is the party of the first part, since the tide rose upon the arrival of the first ship, which has already been graciously unloaded and been refilled with fine Keome products." Yus swept his four arms as he bowed.

"No," Maseer shot back in a much louder voice.

"Stop," Rivka ordered, walking between the two. They continued to glare at each other over her head, and she held up her arms to get their attention. "Time for a break. I will return to my ship with Jay and Red to contemplate the next steps. We shall return in thirty minutes."

Rivka smiled and waved before walking out. A chair had been delivered, but it sat empty. She crooked a finger at a surprised Red, who had been leaning against the wall.

He followed the Magistrate and Jayita to the ship, and once inside they closed the door.

Hamlet yowled for attention and Jay scooped him up on her way to stand in front of the air vent.

Red poured himself a protein shake and drank it down, chasing it with a glass of water.

Rivka went to the bridge to sit alone in the captain's chair. She closed her eyes and reviewed everything that had happened since they'd stepped off the ship.

Everyone lies. The thought kept coming back to her. All parties dealing with the law lied until it was to their disadvantage. Reward the truth and remove the incentive to lie.

The hatred. Sinraloo was as angry as Yutta. She'd seen the flashes when she punched him, but their contact had been too brief. She needed to get Maseer alone. Maybe Yus, too. That was her right as the Magistrate. She'd insist on that after a rewrite of the next nine points.

"Knock them down just like bowling pins," she mused aloud. "Point two. The next shipment comes to Pretaria. How hard is that? If they're going to argue over who's first, then *no one* is first, and all that matters is who's next. If the Keome are lying about having already received a transport, then they will lose that point, because the party of the first part will no longer be in the treaty. Would you boneheads focus on what's important! Chaz, can you confirm whether a Federation transport has made a delivery to this system?"

"Six transports have passed through this system," the EI replied.

"I'll be damned. Show me the arriving and departing manifests."

"There is no difference between the two. The ships did

not transfer any products to either planet although all six ships stopped at both planets."

"You think they would have shared that little fact." Rivka bit her lip as she thought about her next move.

"Rivka?" Red called from the entrance to the bridge.

She rotated one-hundred and eighty degrees because the captain's chair could do that.

"It's been twenty-five minutes."

"Time to go back. Thanks, Red, and I have to say, you look a hell of a lot better."

"I hate the heat."

"And dogs and cats. Fresh wound?"

Red jerked his hand out of sight. "I handed a glass of juice to Jay while she was holding that hellspawned vermin."

"Kitty!" Rivka smiled. She punched Red in the shoulder as she passed and waved to Jay, who was still holding a purring Hamlet. She put him down in the chair, getting scratched for her effort before joining the Magistrate as the hatch opened to the boiling heat.

They hurried inside and toward the conference room. Before they reached it, they found Sinraloo waiting. He wanted to talk with the Magistrate alone.

Rivka leaned against the counter with her arms loosely crossed. The Pretarian's hostility permeated the air, adding to the stifling heat of the small room. Rivka could feel the nanocytes drawing energy to dissipate the heat. She breathed slowly and stayed still to let them do their jobs.

A courtesy she wished Sinraloo would grant her.

After his diatribe and wild arm-waving, he finally paused for breath.

"Are you done?" Rivka asked, straightening herself to leave.

"I haven't even started. The Keome transgressions are numerous, and must be understood if you are to conduct these negotiations in good faith!"

"Stop," she ordered, and held out her hand. He must have been unfamiliar with the gesture since he continued without pause. She tried to get past him, but he barred her way. "Let me by."

He put his back to the door and started a new monologue.

"By order of the Magistrate, you will open that door." She balanced on the balls of her feet and raised her fists. Sinraloo finally stopped talking, but didn't move. "I hold you in violation of Section Thirteen of Federation Code, Chapter Nine, Paragraph Six. Kidnapping."

The Pretarian's expression didn't change. She started to spin, blurring with the speed as she jumped. Her roundhouse kick connected with Sinraloo's jaw, and he started to fall. She hit the floor and followed through with a heel strike from her left hand as his face passed hers. Once he was on the floor, she straddled him and drove her fist toward his nose, stopping before it hit. She grabbed his head in both hands and absorbed his muddled thoughts.

He was too stunned for any of it to be of use. She picked him up, finding the alien much lighter than she would have thought for one of his size and threw him into the wall across the room.

She opened the door and stepped out. Red had his shotgun out and was ready to kick the door in. She looked over her shoulder. "Justice is served, you piece of shit."

Rivka stormed down the hallway until she reached the room set aside for the arbitration. She ripped open the door to find only the Keome delegation.

"Where are the... Never mind. Yus, can I talk to you alone, please?"

He started to walk toward the door, but Yutta stopped him. "How can we know she can be trusted with your safety, Primary Yus?"

"Because she's a Magistrate. The entire planet's safety is in her hands, so I will be safe with her. Why are you so worried?"

"I should come with you," Yutta insisted.

"No." Rivka put her hands on her hips and looked up at the tall multi-armed aliens.

"No," Yus confirmed. He opened the door for Rivka with one arm and held Yutta back with two of his other arms while gesturing with his fourth.

Rivka looked at the two guards. "I need an empty room," she told them. Neither moved nor answered. Red pointed to the bathroom. "It's nice, and no one's in there."

"Good enough." Rivka went in.

Yus took one step and stopped. "But this is a toilet."

"It's a place for privacy, is it not?"

"It is," the Keome conceded before following her in. They didn't bother locking the door since Red was on the other side, barring entry.

"What do you really want from this treaty?" Rivka asked. Yus didn't answer, so she continued, "The treaty as written is a piece of garbage concocted by bureaucrats who want to stab pins into voodoo dolls."

"I don't know what a voodoo doll is, but you are correct in that Keome has an agenda and has tried to force this treaty. They are ready to go to war, you know. Not over this treaty, but to be the supreme power in the system. We call it Keome System and they call it Pretaria System. That alone is enough to go to war over. Whoever names the system determines its fate. Water for us, thirst for them."

"I don't agree, but I see. You still haven't answered my question. Your words represent someone else's position, not yours. You wouldn't be here if you weren't able to speak for your people, so I implore you to answer. What would be acceptable to you?"

"That the Pretarians don't look at me like I am a bug to be squashed."

"That's not asking for a whole lot." Rivka cracked the door. "Red, can you have Maseer join us?"

"He's not here. None of the Pretarian delegation is."

"Tell one of those guards to go get him. I don't know what the hell they're guarding since people are walking around this place as they please."

"Will do, Magistrate," Red replied. Rivka eased the door closed as Red delivered a profanity-laden stream of orders to the two Pretarians on the other side of the hallway.

"You said earlier that you had already traded with the Federation. You and I both know that isn't true. Neither of you has traded anything. Why?"

Yus shuffled one foot. Rivka was learning that the movement was tied to anxiety. Whether angry or upset, it told her something. She had also learned that the tall aliens were patient and slow to speak, and even then, it wasn't because they parsed their words. She waited.

The Primary never answered her, but he stopped shuffling his foot. The door opened slowly and Maseer peeked in.

"Please join us, Maseer," Rivka requested pleasantly, waving the Pretarian forward. He watched Yus closely as he entered and Red shut the door behind him. "We were having what is known as a candid conversation."

Maseer and Yus both looked down on the human.

"In law school and then as an intern, I learned that to get to the core of an issue you have to strip away all the distractions. In the end, it reveals the one thing upon which everything else is built. Sometimes I found that thing was missing, and in a puff of smoke the issue was gone. We have here the three who can make this deal happen. Build it from scratch and implement it in a way that benefits Keome and Pretaria equally."

Neither delegate answered.

"I'll take silence as consent. The best thing to do would be to talk. I think what you have in common is that no one has anything the rest of the universe wants. This trade deal is smoke and mirrors. You have nothing to trade, so as long as the treaty is tied up in this ridiculous feud, you both save face."

"I take exception to that," Maseer argued. "We have something to trade. We are master builders. From the desert, we have formed cities that stand against the wind and the sand." He vigorously bobbed his head, his beads clacking in rhythm with his movements.

"We are also master builders, carving our homes from the cliff faces," Yus countered.

It dawned on Rivka why the Keome had extra limbs and eyes.

"Your export is your people?" Rivka needed to review the diplomatic limitations for the aliens of the system to move around the galaxy. "Is this the foundation we need from which to build the framework for a stronger future?"

"I don't know what you mean," Maseer replied.

Rivka moved to the side so she could "accidentally" brush against Yus. She stayed in contact while gesturing toward Maseer. "The foundation must be strong," she said slowly. Yus angled away from her, but the touch had lasted long enough.

Fear. He was afraid of being killed by his own delegation.

15

Rivka sat in her recliner, rocked back until she was almost horizontal. An old movie played on the screen.

Red had buttoned the ship against all intruders and was relaxing in the recliner next to hers. He snorted and laughed at the show. When she looked at him, he mumbled an apology before resuming his snort-laughing.

Jay was nowhere to be seen. She was probably taking a bath, reveling in the decadence of using so much water.

The Magistrate got up and went to her cabin. She closed the door and enjoyed a few moments of peace and quiet, then a meow shocked her from her reverie. "Hamlet. Don't scratch me."

The cat watched Rivka carefully as the human gave him plenty of room on her way to open the door. He walked to it and sat down in the doorway. She tried to nudge him out with her toe, and he wrapped himself around her shoe and started to gnaw on the sole while scratching madly with his back claws. She tried to shake him free, but he clung to her foot as if part of her shoe.

She laid him on the ground. After he had declared victory over the evil shoe monster, he cleaned his face and headed back into her room.

"No, you get out!" she told him. He vaulted onto her bed and curled up on her pillow. Rivka pulled her chair to the side of the bed so she could stare at him. She locked her eyes on him and stayed there, breathing as loudly as possible. His fur fluffed with each exhale.

After five minutes she gave up and went to the bridge.

She lounged in the captain's chair, leaning back while keeping her eyes on the main screen which showed a view outside the ship. "Chaz, bring up Federation immigration law with any mentions of Pretaria or Keome."

The screen started to scroll. "Start at the beginning." It returned to the top, and she began to read. She heard a thump and found the cat standing on the chair next to her. She'd been out of her room for a grand total of thirty seconds. "What?"

Hamlet started to purr, and he climbed into her lap and curled up. "I'm Magistrate Rivka, and by the power of the Federation, I demand that you obey me or you will be punished to the full extent of the law!"

She scratched his belly. He raised one leg without opening his eyes.

"All that I am, and all that I will ever be, is minion to a cat that doesn't like people. There's my epitaph. Note that, Chaz and continue to scroll—slowly, please. Stop. What is that I see?" She started to lean forward but caught herself before upsetting Hamlet.

"Nice. Continue scrolling." Absentmindedly she stroked the cat's soft fur, and he started to purr even though she would have sworn he was asleep. Brighter thoughts raced through her mind and made her smile. "I love the law."

The morning heat was as oppressive as the mid-day sun. Both sought to destroy human life by reducing it to cinders. The Magistrate's team hurried from the ship to the building, finding that one type of heat had been replaced by another.

"Did they turn off the a/c or what?" Jay asked. Red started to flush, and he splashed a canteen over his head to expedite the cooling. He had already drunk his fill aboard the ship. Rivka led the way through the inner doors and down the hall toward the meeting room. When they arrived, there were no guards or delegates. Inside, the conference table had been righted and returned to the center of the room.

"What time do you have, Red?"

"I have that we are right on time."

"Jay, any thoughts?"

"Lots of them, but none are good. This looks like a setup. If I were back on the station, I'd be running for my life right about now."

Rivka thought of her pink hair flowing behind her. She had changed it at Rivka's request, and it was now a golden blond that seemed to suit the young woman better. It was the same length and would flow behind her when she ran, regardless.

"Good call. We're out of here. We can call them from the ship to find out what happened."

Rivka walked quickly toward the door, but when she pushed through it she found the two guards in the entry area. They had their weapons in hand, although they weren't aiming them.

"You have no need of your weapons with us," the Magistrate told them.

"We were instructed by Lead Maseer to make sure you remained, since the delegation was unavoidably detained."

"I'm sure holding us hostage wasn't what Maseer had in mind. And what about the Keome?" Rivka inched toward the guards.

"What *about* the Keome?" the upstart asked.

Rivka used her enhanced speed to cover the last meter to the guards, ripping their weapons from their hands before they could react. Red had his shortened shotgun up and aimed at the head of the closer Pretarian. Rivka held the weapons behind her for Jay to take.

"Why did you detain us?" She grabbed the guard's arm and held it. He tried to pull away, but she was stronger. His emotions flashed through her mind. Foremost was fear, but the images were jumbled. She had yet to figure out how to parse the alien memories. He had no family that she could tell. His existence was based on his duty, and he felt like he was failing.

A spy! Rivka removed her hand, immediately wanting to return to the ship and wash with bleach.

"Call us when Maseer and Yus have arrived." Jay was first to the door, with Rivka close behind. Red held his shotgun close to the guard's face as he passed.

"Try something, shit stain. I want to see how Pretarian brains splatter." The guards did not give him the opportunity, just remained motionless until after Vered had backed through the front doors and raced into the ship.

The hatch closed, but Red continued to aim his shotgun at it.

"I think we're good," Rivka suggested.

"What in the hell is up with these dickweeds? I can't figure them out, which gives them the upper hand. I hate that."

"And dogs, and cats, and the heat. Next time, we're going to request a special parking spot just for you."

Red pointed at the deck. "What do you call this?"

"The deck?"

"A parking spot right next to the building. You're welcome," he told her as he slung his shotgun over his shoulder and headed for the lounge.

Rivka couldn't argue. She took the captain's chair on the bridge while the others went about their business, efficiently killing time until being called back into action.

"Chaz..." she started to say before he interrupted her.

"You have an incoming video communication from Maseer."

"Onscreen," she directed in a low and commanding voice.

"Magistrate! Good to see you. We must have just missed you, like two desert schooners passing in the night."

"I'm sure it was just a minor mix-up where the clocks of your entire delegation failed you all simultaneously. No matter. Call us when the Keome delegation arrives, and then I need both of you to wait for us in the lobby. Thank you." She signed off before they could respond.

"Chaz..."

"You have an incoming video communication from Yus."

"Onscreen."

"We are here, and you are not. We won't be trifled with!" he shouted at the screen.

Rivka angled her head. She hadn't expected such theatrics. His eyes darted to the side and back to the screen. "We were there on time and left one minute after the appointed meeting start time. I will not tolerate further obstructionism from Keome! I am on my way in right now."

She didn't want to come across as too demanding; make it look like she was forcing Keome to be subservient. Let him save face.

"Time to go," she yelled toward the lounge. Red and Jay both appeared. Red held his shotgun, and Jay had one of the two guards' weapons. "What are you going to do with that?"

"Protect myself?" she answered with a question. "These people seem pretty hostile. It's like they are channeling their anger away from each other and onto us."

"The enemy of my enemy," Rivka offered. "Leave the weapon here, please. I need you focused on them. Your idea to share water was a great way to break the ice, not that there is any ice on this planet. We need to start each day that way."

She motioned toward the hatch, and Red took his cue and dove headlong into the heat. He marched quickly across the intervening space and went inside, then stuck one hand back out and gave the thumbs-up.

"Showtime," Rivka decreed.

The two delegations stood as far as possible from each other. Rivka walked into the open area in between. "Would you share water with me?" she asked.

Jay produced a number of thin steel stackable glasses and started to pour. No one else moved. She half-filled the glasses as the Pretarians had done when they first arrived. Rivka thanked her and picked up one glass.

"Will you join me?"

The two delegations stood like statues, unflinching in their resolve.

Rivka fought back her growing anger. She took a sip of the water, let it run over her tongue. Then she drank the remainder and turned the glass over as she returned it to the small table. She started to pace slowly, with her hands clasped behind her back. Red leaned against the entry door and watched the delegations, wondering where the two security guards had gone. Jay studied the aliens, looking for their tells.

"Travel requires movement, which starts by putting one foot in front of another. How long are we going to stand here? You are both wasting all of our time. This grandstanding accomplishes nothing, except forcing me to exercise my further rights under the Law of Arbitration. I am designating a single delegate from each party. I will work with those two only, in private, until the arbitration is complete. This is the only way we move forward. If you want to go fast, go alone. If you want to go far, go together. Well, my esteemed colleagues from Pretaria and Keome, we are about to go far."

The foot-shuffling began.

Rivka took another glass of water and drank it. She swapped the empty for another full glass and strolled up to Sinraloo. "How's that jaw?" she asked him and walked to the Keome. She looked at Yutta. "How's that gut? I didn't hurt you too badly, did I?"

The Keome loomed over her. "You surprised me."

"As you surprised me. No one expects to get barbarically attacked while on an official mission and in formal diplomatic chambers. That does not reflect well on your people."

She walked back to the open space.

"Yus and Maseer, we will go to my corvette. That is where the arbitration will take place. Follow me."

"No, wait," Yus said. He pointed at the door to the conference room.

"Absolutely not. My ship. Now." She held the door and the heat entered in waves. Red grimaced and moved farther into the room. Jay picked up the glasses and poured the water back into the jug, then replaced everything in her carry bag.

Rivka glared at the two delegations. "I will give you five seconds before I hold you both in contempt. I didn't come here to deliver punishment, but you've already forced me to twice judge lawbreakers. Is that going to be you, too? Do you even know what you signed when you joined the Federation?" She shuffled a foot in the way the aliens did.

She began her countdown "Five. Four." She moved closer to Maseer. "Three." She grabbed him by the front of his shirt and yanked him nearly out of his boots. "Two." She started to drag him across the room. Yus stepped back. "Come here, criminal," she growled. "One." She lunged forward and grabbed Yus. She propelled both of the tall aliens toward the door with as much shove as she could manage.

They both stumbled two steps and stopped.

"FREEZE!" Red roared and slapped the handgrip of his shotgun.

Sinraloo and Yutta, Rivka thought. She bit her lip to keep herself from laughing. *Freeze,* on a planet where the average temperature was that of a good cup of coffee.

"Go!" she ordered. The two aliens exited the building, and Rivka backed out after them. She didn't take her eyes from the room until she was outside. Red signaled for Jay to precede him. When he reached the door, Red fired into the ceiling and ran out.

"Woohoo!" he shouted as he vaulted up the short stairs and through the hatch. "Just like Koreanis Four. Hot damn!" He secured the hatch and turned to find Rivka scowling.

"Well, it was," he muttered softly.

She snickered. "'Freeze?'"

"What?" he shot back, standing up straight and throwing his shoulders back.

"Talking about freezing, get our guests a couple of coats, please."

"No can do. Busy guarding the boss." Red remained where he was.

"That ship has sailed. These two are no threat. You dealt with the ones we need to worry about."

"But, keep your friends close and your enemies closer?" Red wondered.

"Not in this case. These two are our friends, and they will make this work. Now go get a couple of coats. I'm sure they are freezing in here."

"Already taken care of, Magistrate," Jay told her. Rivka turned left at the corner between the bridge and the mess deck. Maybe it was the lounge. More likely the negotiation chamber.

The tall aliens squatted on the low human-sized chairs as they huddled with two heavy blankets wrapped around their shoulders. They were still shivering from the brief time they had been on board before Jay took care of them.

Rivka sat in front of them, leaning forward to study the two delegates. "Gentlemen. This is where the magic will happen. The spies who are listening to your every word have been removed from the equation. We can work in the peace and serenity of my ship. The ship with no name," she added.

It wouldn't make a good plaque. *The Treaty to end all treaties was signed on this spot aboard Corvette Seven Seven Four.*

"The *Peacemaker*. The *Arbinator*," Jay offered softly. Rivka looked at the floor and closed her eyes to better gather her thoughts.

"My name is Yus. I come from Ekmone, from family Ekmone. I am here because Keome didn't want someone they could trust. They wanted someone they could control.

My family is at risk if I don't come back with a treaty that denigrates Pretaria and awards all trade to Keome."

"All?" Rivka asked, wondering at the extreme nature of the word.

"*All*. Which is impossible, of course, as my Pretarian counterpart will confirm."

They both looked to Maseer. "I am Maseer, and I am the Primary of Pretaria. I speak for my people. They know not what is best for them, but they will mob the government if we do not put Keome in its place. I am in charge, but not in charge of anything. No Primary ever has been. We are elected by a popular vote that is readily manipulated even though the winner matters not, since nothing will change unless those in charge want to change it. The business and religious leaders call the shots."

"Your businesses are stymied without Federation trade. Expand to the universe and see what's possible."

"Our people think they want what Keome has."

Yus watched Maseer closely. "We have nothing anyone wants, which is why Keome wants what you have."

"It appears that the grass is greener on the other side of the fence—until you get there and find that it is not, and never has been." Rivka stood up and waved at the screen. "Chaz, if you would be so kind, please bring up my notes from last night."

Federation law appeared in its tight and small font, while a larger window highlighted the key points.

"Interesting," Yus and Maseer said together.

16

Red volunteered to go, but Rivka wouldn't let him. "We'll call it in. Nothing like some good takeout. It'd be great if it weren't toxic to humans, so we'll settle for good and eat our own slop."

Red tried not to look offended.

"What would you like to eat, gentlemen?" Rivka interrupted. The Pretarian and the Keome were head-down, jamming an entirely new treaty that Rivka would declare her work and force both parties to comply with while secretly knowing that the representatives had crafted a treaty together—something that was in their own best interests.

They had reduced the number of points from forty-seven to ten, whittling away the incessant denigration that each society had demanded and focusing solely on what each society needed. The upper hand? Neither had that.

"Are you sure?" Maseer asked.

"Researched, double-checked, and verified," Rivka replied. She gave him the thumbs-up.

"Human gestures are so very odd." Maseer tried to replicate the gesture by holding up two of his five fingers and failed.

"I agree. It is both stultifying and mesmerizing."

Rivka nodded. "What do you want to eat? I'll order you something, since our food units don't make anything you can eat."

"Turbid Pie, please," Yus said without hesitation.

"I think we have something similar. I'll take that, too, please."

"Coming right up." Rivka returned to the bridge. "Chaz, show me the definition of the word 'stultifying.'"

"1: Cause to appear foolish. 2: Render ineffectual by degrading means. 3: Allege or prove to be of unsound mind (legal)."

"I'll be damned. I think I'll have to use that word more, especially as it relates to Grainger. Thanks, Chaz. Please call the Pretarians and have two orders of Turbid Pie delivered to the ship, quick as they can."

"Of course, Magistrate," the EI replied pleasantly.

"Connect me with Grainger, please."

The interstellar communications device tapped through the ship's systems. The miniaturized Etheric power supply helped it connect instantly.

"Nethers. Is it war? Do we need to deploy the fleet? The end of all life as we know it? Or are you stuck and need a sage and guiding hand?"

"That is so very stultifying. You should be *ashamed*!"

"You think I'm of unsound mind? I can't imagine what I

have or haven't done to earn that label, but I'll take it! It's much better than Schlong-Man, a most unsavory alternative. But I am interrupting. Pray tell, what brings your feather-soft words to my undeserving ears?"

"You have to be one of the weirdest individuals I've ever met. To your most undeserving ears, I deliver unto thee my status report."

"Shoot," Grainger encouraged.

"Both sides lied, and their treaty was a total pile of garbage. We're rewriting it in its entirety. I expect to have signatures on it later today or first thing tomorrow."

"Everybody lies!" Grainger exclaimed. "That's our first assumption whenever we talk to these people. I thought I hired a raging bull and methinks we have a naive school girl instead."

"You are such a bawdy fuckwit-fondler. When I get back, with the crisis successfully avoided and the treaty intact, you will buy me a beer. On a completely different note, since we are talking about someone looking foolish, you have to give Red some nanocytes. He is susceptible to heat like you can't believe. Walked a hundred meters in this blast furnace and keeled over like a dead cactus. I had to carry his big ass into the first meeting. I don't mean arm-over-my-shoulder, either. Fireman's carry. I should get a bonus for that."

"You should! Too bad you won't. I'll consider Pod-doc time for Red, but we'll have to tie him to a long-term contract. Can't have people trained to his degree getting enhanced and then being turned loose upon the universe. I think he'll probably be fine, but I want to be sure before we do. Can you get into his head and check?"

"I don't like doing that," she replied.

The silence was pure. There were no errant crackles or pops. The only sound on the bridge was the gentle hum of the air-handling system. It was warmer than they usually liked it, but still about eighty degrees cooler than the aliens were used to.

"It is completely your call. Just let me know when you get back, and we'll dial him up a set of hot pants."

"I don't think that means what you think it means. He did tell them to freeze, though, so he wouldn't have to shoot them."

"Was that before or after you carried him?"

"After..." she drew the word out, wondering what Grainger was thinking. It didn't take long.

"You tell Chilly Willy we'll hook him up." Rivka snorted. "Anything else?"

"How are you doing on *your* mission? And the others?"

"I'll be damned if Cheese Blintz isn't already back. It took him less than an hour to break down the crime and catch the perp. When you have nine suspects and a small area within which to work, it makes things easier."

"What about Jael?"

"She's chasing ghosts. The deeper she digs, the more bodies she finds. It's giving her more to work with, and still dead ends. It's not going well. The people are afraid."

"Understandable," Rivka agreed.

"I'm on Yoll. Still." Grainger didn't share anything further.

"I see how you are. I'll take the high road and be home long before you. Magistrate Rivka Anoa, out." She signed off. The others were fighting the good fight, but Chi was already back, maybe out on another mission already. There was no end to lawlessness.

"ETA on chow, Chaz?"

"If I didn't know better, I would think you were speaking in tongues," the EI replied. "The food for our delegates will arrive in sixty standard minutes."

"Another hour? Are they making it from scratch?"

"I am led to believe it is a lengthy process. Turbid Pie is considered a delicacy and is very expensive. I have charged the cost to your card, Magistrate."

Rivka's face fell. "This is how it's going to be, huh?" She pulled herself from the captain's chair. It wasn't as comfortable as the recliner, but the aliens had that blocked. Their tall bodies, wrapped with blankets, seemed to completely fill the space on the mess deck.

Rivka leaned against the bulkhead and watched the aliens work. The white cat was coming from the short corridor where the cabins were located. He looked at the veritable mountains in the middle of the room and hissed before sniffing. He jumped onto the blanket and started climbing upward. Yus looked over his shoulder, and his eyes shot wide as plates when he saw the cat. He bolted upright, throwing the blanket from his shoulders.

He slammed into the overhead and crumpled to the deck. Hamlet shot into the corner, dashed over him, turned sideways, and finally bolted back toward the crew's cabins. Maseer was petrified by fear.

"Primary?" Rivka called as she waved a hand in front of his face. "Are you going to be okay?"

"I have never been so terrified. You have a creature on board your ship?"

Rivka checked the bump on Yus' head.

"A cat. His name is Hamlet. There are those who say they are the greatest predator in the universe, but since they're only five kilos, they're perpetually pissed off. He's also very cuddly."

"Cuddly? I don't know this word."

"I feel sorry for all Pretarians." She sat on the floor cradling the Keome's head while Jay draped the blanket over him again. "And I think all Keome, too. It'll be an hour before the Turbid Pie arrives. I hope you don't mind."

"An hour." Maseer kept his eyes fixed on the corridor down which the cat disappeared. "I hope they aren't taking shortcuts. It is a delicate process to make the dish properly. One hour is barely enough time."

"Hamlet is one of my crew," Rivka told him as Yus started to stir.

"You keep a terrifying creature as one of your crew? What is its role?"

Rivka opened her mouth to defend Hamlet, but the words didn't come. Red and Jay both held up hands showing razor thin scabs where they'd been scratched. Her claw marks had healed, thanks to the power of the nanocytes.

"Advanced combat techniques with non-bipedal life forms. He's also my ship's morale officer."

"Morale?"

"Yes. He makes me happy because he makes Red sad."

"I'm not sad..." Red started to say.

Jay punched him before blurting, "I love him!"

Yus spasmed as he sat up. He twisted his head back and forth and up and down as he looked for his enemy.

"Relax," Rivka told him. "I should have mentioned Hamlet. He's not as terrifying as all that. You don't have cats, clearly. Do you keep pets at all?"

"Pets? I don't know the word. We have no mammals on Keome besides us. We have insects, of course, hexapod invertebrates being the most prevalent, but nothing like that horrendous creature." Yus snaked a hand from under his blanket to point down the corridor Maseer continued to watch.

"Where did it go? Will it come back?"

"He. His name is Hamlet, and he lives here. Jay, can you bring him out?"

Jayita put her hands on her hips. "He's a little bit scared right now, and I'm not a fan of donating my flesh and blood for a group hug."

Rivka could not disagree. "He is my friend," Rivka began. "Even though he's only been in my life for a couple days, I am happier for it. Same with you two. I know what you are both struggling with. For some insane reason, your two societies want to hate each other. People with nothing looking across the fence and thinking that the other guy has something they don't. Neither of your planets has anything, but they have everything they need to thrive. I'm not talking handouts. I'm talking about being able to make your own way. Leave envy behind, since it does neither of you any good."

Maseer finally looked away from the corridor. "But my people..." His thought stopped.

Yus looked down at the blanket. "I think I can get up," he told Rivka, who had continued to cradle his head in her lap. The tall alien unwound his long arms and legs from the blanket, stood, and then rewrapped it around him. "I can't believe how cold you prefer it. I would think your bodies would stop moving and freeze in place. The heat is such a wonderful lubricant for the joints. You should try it."

Red didn't look like he agreed.

"There is someone outside the ship with a delivery."

"Turbid Pie!" the delegates said in unison.

"I'll get it," Red told them, not inviting argument. He reached into a pack that he kept in the common room and pulled out something that Rivka hadn't seen before. "No bugs."

"That could be a problem, because Turbid Pie is made from the largest of the hexapods."

"Not *that* kind of bug. Listening devices, although I suspect that Chaz can prevent any emissions from inside the ship. We have a power source that helps the ship to do many unexpected things."

The group cleared the small counter in the kitchen while they waited for Red to return. He put the box in the empty spot and held up two small devices. "Someone doesn't like not knowing what's going on."

"One from each of our delegations?" Maseer suggested.

"Probably. It looks like they may be starting to agree on something—that they can't control us." Yus passed the first of two boxes to Maseer, who thanked him and waited for Yus to get his own. They opened them together.

"Smells just like Mom used to make."

"Me, too," Yus agreed.

Rivka stifled a gag. Red swallowed hard. Jay was nowhere to be seen.

"I'll be on the bridge," Rivka told them.

"I'll be somewhere else," Red added.

The delegates never realized that the others had left since they were consumed with the delicacy. They ate it standing up, savoring every bite.

"I think we're ready to share the new treaty with both your worlds. Now that the framework is established, what are the next steps?"

"Since we've demanded arbitration, our respective governments have to simply accept what is written. There is no opportunity to dispute the treaty. This will cause many of our people to get upset," Maseer explained.

"The time to get upset was before requesting that the Federation get involved. What I mean is, what will they do to you?"

Maseer looked at Yus.

"Me? My family will probably be in prison before the day is out, and when I return, I shall join them."

"I fear my fate will be similar. We agree, my friend Yus and I, that we will be vindicated in time. We may never see it, but this is the right thing to do for both our planets if we are ever to move forward. Joining the Federation was a great thing, but each of our planets had a selfish reason to do so. It was the right thing to do, but for the wrong reason. This treaty changes that."

"And you will both be punished for doing right by your people." Rivka sighed heavily. People made sacrifices all the time, for their families or for their beliefs. Martyrs for the cause. She knew it was the right thing to do, but she couldn't agree with letting the two delegates shoulder the burden. "How can we convince them that this is my document and you argued violently against it?"

"We are the ones who will have to sign it. Our signatures will be our final words."

"You *don't* have to sign it. Maybe we do it that way. You refuse, but the arbitration will be complete and enforceable under Federation law. No, you will both refuse to sign it."

She looked from one to the other. She had to know, so Rivka touched Yus' arm, held it for a moment, then touched Maseer.

A spark of hope springing from a black pit of sadness. Their thoughts were nearly identical. They were both willing to give their lives for what they believed in, but it made Rivka sad that they thought that way. Trade agreements shouldn't be life or death for their champions.

"Your worlds could not have selected better representatives. Maybe there is hope for all of Intripas. I am honored to have worked with you." She turned toward the bridge. "Chaz, please inform the official representatives from both delegations that we will be joining them in the conference room momentarily."

"It is late at night," Yus exclaimed.

Rivka frowned. "Does anyone know what day it is?"

Red waited in the corridor. Two guards were stationed there, different from the ones from whom Rivka had taken the weapons. Jay and Rivka sat in the conference room chairs with their legs dangling. The delegates sat on their respective sides of the table. Their heads were in their hands, and they both looked to be asleep.

"We should have brought Hamlet with us. He would have made things exciting."

"Can cats survive heat like this?" Rivka wondered. "And no, we can't terrorize the locals with all five kilos of our little killer."

Jay chuckled. Rivka jumped down and started to pace. She hadn't realized how tired she was until she stopped moving. "I should have waited until morning, but if we can wrap this up now, then we can go home. I have beer waiting for me."

"And me," Jay added.

"You're not old enough yet. Shirley Temples for you, but you can join us. You're my crew."

The door opened and remaining members of both delegations forced their way into the room, snarling at each other as they hurried to their respective leaders. They all talked at once, but Yus called for calm and Maseer followed suit.

Rivka yelled, "Shut it!" She jumped back into the chair and then stood on it to be at eye level with the tallest of the aliens. "This is the treaty that I'm going to force down your throats. Both Maseer and Yus have refused to sign, and I don't care. Their signatures are not required for this treaty to be binding on both your people. Take a few minutes to read what I am committing you to."

The room turned deathly silent. Yus slid his pad to the side to allow the delegation to read it. Maseer handed his to Rhonali, his deputy. Each side started reading, snorting and grunting as if they were undergoing the trials of Job.

"I'll sign it," Maseer whispered. "On behalf of all Pretaria."

"As will I," Yus said. "Keome comes to this in the best interests of its people."

The delegations started yelling, filling the room with noise. Rivka could not make out individual conversations. Yus held his head where the bump from his impact with the ceiling was barely visible. Maseer stood, and then sat, too tired to fight the others. He looked at the table and tried to tune them out.

Jay dove off her chair and Rivka turned, wondering what she was doing. The bomb exploded from somewhere near Yus. The table heaved upward, throwing both delegations into the walls.

Why? Rivka thought as her body was flying into the ceiling on its way to the wall, ending with darkness on the floor.

17

Red held her eyelid open. She tried to blink, but he had it solidly in place.

"Thank God you're alive," he said before letting go. She finally mashed her eyelid closed and blinked the world back into focus. Her tear ducts worked to flush the dust and debris. "How long?"

"Seconds. The bomb went off less than a minute ago."

"Damage?" she asked as she tried to get up. Red held her down.

"Yus is dead, and the others are pretty fucked up."

"Jay!" Rivka rolled her head as she tried to see past the massive body of her guard. Jayita's face appeared at Red's elbow. Rivka nodded, which sent a wave of pain through her brain. "You saw it. What happened?"

"A box appeared beneath Yus' hands. It came out of nowhere. I hadn't seen anything like it since we arrived. I'm sorry." The young woman started sobbing.

Red looked over his shoulder. The guards were coordinating the assistance that was starting to arrive. They removed the first delegate, carrying him to the hall.

"Don't cry," Rivka told her firmly as her head stopped throbbing. She chalked it up to the nanos racing through her system to repair the damage. "Someone tried to kill us. We will find out who, using the law as our sword and shield, and then Justice will be served. No one brings a bomb into my house. *No one.*"

Red helped her to her feet. The conference room was wrecked, debris from the table scattered throughout and the walls painted with blood. Maseer was unconscious. Rivka kneeled by his side and watched a Pretarian she didn't know wrap a brace around his neck. The alien glanced at her with angry eyes before returning to her work.

Rivka felt helpless. The Pretarians brought stretchers to carry the five members of the Pretarian delegation. They had workers bandaging and helping the Keome, but they were going to be moved second. Miento, Yus' secondary, was horribly injured. Sinraloo was barely scratched, yet had been carried out first.

"Grab her feet," Rivka ordered. One of the Pretarians started to protest but decided it was best to step aside. Red wrapped his arms under the victim's legs. On three they lifted, taking care to keep her steady. They hurried out, following the stretcher carrying Sinraloo. He started shaking a fist at them.

"You better not be shaking that at me," she shouted. He laid back, but never took his eyes from the Magistrate. She glared back. *Your days are numbered, you bastard. You are Suspect Number One.*

She wished he could hear her thoughts.

A line of stretchers waited at an elevator. It arrived, and two more went in. Sinraloo and Miento were next. "Looks like we have the same ride," Rivka told him.

He finally looked away and closed his eyes. The two carrying his stretcher appeared to be uncomfortable but didn't engage the Magistrate's withering gaze. "Since we have a few moments, Sinraloo, what did you see in there right before the blast?"

The Pretarian slowly opened his eyes.

"Red."

"My bodyguard was in the corridor," she replied, confused by his answer.

"Not the minion, the color. Fury from the grossly unjust trade agreement you are foisting on us! The Federation..." He let the word hang as if it were poison.

"Who brought the box with the bomb, Sinraloo? My first guess is that it was you. Your answer suggests it was you. I could declare you guilty right now and mete out punishment. Would you like that, Sinraloo, being condemned to death for your crimes and then on top of it, getting your ass beaten by an ice-veined human?"

"Even with my low regard for the Federation, I don't think you'd condemn an innocent. For the record, it wasn't me."

"Then tell me what you saw." Rivka wanted to touch him to see the truth, but her hands were full with the Keome.

"Red." Sinraloo's eyes remained closed. The elevator arrived, and four Pretarians rushed out carrying two empty stretchers. Sinraloo's bearers headed into the elevator first. The nearest Pretarian blocked the entry. Red elbowed him in the side.

"Make room," Red growled and forced his way in. Miento groaned with the jostling. The elevator ride was tense, with the humans glaring at the Pretarians and Miento's pain causing her more and more anguish.

When the elevator stopped Rivka went first out, blocking the exit until Red cleared it. She looked over her shoulder to see where she was going, walking quickly backward until she entered the ad hoc infirmary set up in what looked to be a dining facility. They laid Miento on the next open table. A Pretarian acting as an orderly pointed to the other side of the hall where there were fewer people and no equipment.

Rivka puffed out her chest and stood between the Pretarian and the Keome and the alien soon walked away. There was no space for Sinraloo. The stretcher bearers stood there looking at the table on which Miento lay.

"Take him over there." Rivka pointed to the side that was set up to provide minimal care. "There's nothing wrong with his candy ass that can't be handled over there. She needs the best care you can provide."

Sinraloo spoke. "We don't care for the Keome, not in the way you are demanding. We will provide minimal medical assistance, only enough to keep them alive."

Rivka thought for a moment. "I think she's dying. She needs assistance."

"The doctors will determine that," Sinraloo replied, keeping his eyes closed and looking like he was asleep. "In due time."

Rivka and Red waited, relegated to the role of observers. "Make sure no one dies. I need to think."

Red grimaced, keeping Rivka between him and the wall as he spoke over his shoulder. "Not sure how I'm supposed to do that, but I'll do my best to keep you from dying, although that's turned into a total shit show. I expect I'll be fired when we get back."

"Not if I have anything to say about it," Rivka replied without looking up from her datapad. She continued, but Red knew that she wasn't speaking to him. "Planetary law is superior in local issues, and in regard to immigration Federation law would supersede, except these two planets are in the same system. Federation law contemplates this situation through separate agreements but... Precedent. The courts were designed to be an intermediate body between the people and the legislature, in order, among other things, to keep the latter within the limits assigned to their authority."

Alexander Hamilton, Rivka thought. So old, but telling of a higher purpose—creating a legal buffer between the governed and those who govern, with separate and ultimate authority in the interpretation of the law.

"I don't see anything we can do," Rivka whispered as she put a hand on Red's shoulder and watched the first two stretchers arrive with the Keome. Two Pretarians picked Miento up from the table and moved her to the other side of the room. Sinraloo got up from his table and moved to the spot, waiting for another to wipe it off before he laid down. He never took his eyes from Rivka.

She clenched her jaw so tightly her face shook. She

wanted to scream. The law was her friend, until it wasn't. But no amount of fist-shaking would change the here and now. She looked back to her pad. Pulled up the treaty. It was less than four hundred words. At the end of the clause on equal treatment, she added, "Injured sentient creatures, regardless of origin, shall be treated in order of medical priority. Any deaths shall be subject to Federation review and the treatment center subject to sanction for misprioritization, as determined by competent Federation medical authority."

She pressed her thumb to it and hit transmit.

"Maybe not the cleanest legal language, but challenge it, and I'll see you in court. Welcome to your new commitment to the Federation, motherfuckers," she snarled loud enough for Sinraloo to hear.

With her second mission completed—implementing an agreement arrived at under arbitration—Rivka started her new case: find the perp and bring him, her, or them to Justice.

She, Red, and Jay had returned to the conference room, secured it, and started searching.

"I should have paid more attention in my forensics class," Rivka told them as she sifted through the bloody debris. "The crime scene is contaminated."

Red stayed less than an arm's length from Rivka at all times. He continued to express his remorse in not protecting her from the bomb by failing to keep it from entering the conference room.

"Trust aliens to do my job, and this is what I get," he lamented.

"Let it go, Red." Rivka put a hand on his arm, only to be pummeled by his thoughts of self-recrimination. He was ashamed. She stepped back, wound up a haymaker, and swung for his head. He ducked out of reach.

"What the hell are you doing?"

"Meting out punishment. You won't forgive yourself, so let's get this over with so we can get back to work."

Red cocked his head and smiled. "Make it good." He leaned forward and closed his eyes.

Rivka kissed him on one cheek while gently slapping the other. "Justice is served. Now find me that fucking bomb."

Red looked confused, but Rivka waved him away and returned to digging into the debris. Blood mixed with dust had made a plaster and clumped disparate pieces together. She used a splinter from the table to separate the components.

"There were eleven datapads in the room. I have mine. Where are the other ten?"

"I thought we were looking for a box?" Red asked.

"If we eliminate all the electronics from pads, then whatever is left will be part of the bomb."

"What if they were carrying other stuff with them—communicators or key rings or who knows what?" Jay suggested.

Rivka wasn't pleased with the idea. "We have to start somewhere, and that is the best I got," she said in a tired voice.

"I'm not finding any datapads," Red told them. "Or electronic keychains, for that matter."

"The perps cleaned everything up. A conspiracy?" Rivka wondered.

"Had to be the Pretarians. The Keome were in no shape to remove anything."

"Sinraloo," Rivka snarled. "I need to touch him. It would help if I had evidence to back me up, but it's not critical. Complete the search, then we're off to the hospital. I want to talk with Maseer, and I need to offer a helping hand to Sinraloo."

When Rivka, Red, and Jay walked from the conference room, they found two guards waiting for them.

"We're to escort you wherever you go," the one told them emotionlessly.

"Fine. Are you guys any better than the two who allowed a bomb into that room?" Rivka pointed. The Pretarians didn't answer.

The injured had been transferred to a hospital, which was attached by a tube train to the complex in which the conference room was located. One guard led the way, with Red at his side. The other guard brought up the rear while Rivka and Jay walked in the middle.

"Can't see anything," Jay complained.

"Such is the life of a DV. A distinguished visitor." Rivka fought to keep her emotions under control. She was raging mad at the Pretarians for their treatment of the Keome, but none of the others had died. Only Yus, because the blast had happened right under his nose. Even with her quick addition to the treaty, the Federation would not have been able to intervene in any review of the Pretarian actions following the explosion.

They need to be put in their place, but I can't wish for someone to die so I can beat the Pretarians over the head because of their mindless bigotry.

Rivka scowled as she walked. When they arrived at the train platform, she found it incongruent with what she'd seen elsewhere in the complex. It was colorfully decorated and teeming with life.

"Maybe there's hope for the Pretarians after all."

Red signaled for Rivka to stop as he backed up close to her. A contingent of Pretarians started chanting as they approached, shoulder to shoulder to block Rivka's way.

"There she is! Keome-lover. *Keome-lover*," they yelled in unison.

"Let me talk with them, Red," Rivka asked, but the big man wouldn't let her by. "Let me shout over your shoulder, then."

Red dipped his leg so she could stand on his calf and see the crowd before her. "I love Pretarians, too!" she yelled.

They continued, unconvinced.

"I have a cat named Hamlet. He'd make you all run for your lives, all five kilos of him. Please allow me to pass so I can find who bombed your delegation."

They weren't listening.

She turned to the stoic guard beside her. "I need to get to the hospital."

"It doesn't look like you're going to make it," he replied. The guard behind her adopted the same pose.

"I wonder how they'll react to loud noises?" Rivka whispered into Red's ear before hopping down.

Red checked the overhead, pulled his shotgun, and fired into an area devoid of pipes and cables. The chanting finally stopped.

Rivka dodged from behind her bodyguard and started to shout. "I am a Federation Magistrate on official business. You will disperse, or face the course of Justice."

"You will go home!" a bold Pretarian yelled back. Rivka strolled forward.

"Dammit!" Red muttered, but he stayed right behind her, his shotgun aimed over her head at the angry alien line.

Rivka approached the vocal member of the crowd.

"What makes you so angry?"

"The agreement! There *was* no agreement. We didn't sign it, so we are not obligated to follow it. You have no authority here, now go away."

"Is that what you're being told? That it is patently wrong. Your government joined the Federation, and your government requested Federation arbitration." She pointed to herself. "That's me. If Pretaria wanted to simply hate the Keome, Pretaria should have gone to war with them without signing a treaty."

The Pretarian thought for a moment. "Down with Keome!"

"Protesting is your right. I judge that to be within the law, but preventing me from investigating a crime is illegal. You will allow me to pass."

"Go home!"

"Three," Rivka began. A train was approaching the

station, and some of the Pretarians left the protest to get in line to board.

"Two." The train pulled in, but the remaining Pretarians blocked her way.

"One." They held their ground.

Rivka jump-kicked the speaker in the chest, followed by punches to the left and right. A hole had been created, and Red plowed into the fray.

"Come on, Jay!" Rivka yelled from the front as she ran for a train car's open door. Jay skipped by the guard and accelerated. She grabbed Red's jacket as he butt-stroked another Pretarian with his shotgun. When he and Jay jumped into the car, Rivka stepped across the threshold.

She turned back to see the chaos on the platform.

Red studied the Pretarian faces on the car. All of them were watching the humans. He wiped the sweat from his face with a sleeve.

"I'm not sure you endeared yourself to them," Jay whispered.

"History will show that their hatred was wrong, but in the interim, let me be the lightning rod. If they can't respect the Magistrate, let them fear her." Rivka held her head high and returned the aliens' stares until they looked away.

"Do you know where we're going?" Jay asked.

Rivka pointed at the receding platform. "I was following them." The guards and those remaining on the platform disappeared as the train eased around a corner.

Jay smiled at the nearest Pretarian. "Can you tell us the way to the hospital?" She waited. "Please?"

Nothing.

"You'd think with all this heat lubricating their joints they'd be more talkative," Red offered while keeping his eyes on the others in the car.

Rivka saw that he was still cradling his shotgun. "Put that thing away." She shook her head and accessed her datapad. The map that the Pretarians had provided ended at the train platform. "I'm getting a bad feeling about this."

"What's the plan, boss?" Red asked.

Rivka blew out a breath. "Off at the next station, and we'll go from there."

The train started to slow. "Is this the right time to point out that your plan sucks?"

"Tell me something I don't know," Rivka replied, shifting her weight onto the balls of her feet and clenching and unclenching her fists.

"They shouldn't have poked the bear," Jay suggested.

18

Rivka walked off the train, smiling congenially. Red walked at her shoulder, head swiveling. The Pretarians stared but didn't get in her way.

"Looks like word has already spread," Rivka remarked, continuing to smile as she walked. "Does anyone see any signs?"

"None," Jay replied. Red didn't look for signs. He only watched the Pretarians.

"There's one who doesn't look like he hates us." Red pointed with his chin at an elderly alien, slumped, and barely taller than Red.

Rivka made a beeline for her. "Can you tell us where the hospital is?" she asked. The old Pretarian pointed with a skeletal hand toward a nearby walkway. "Thank you."

Rivka walked in that direction. "How do you know she's not leading you into a trap?"

"Worse than the last one our supposed guards walked us into? Or into a conference room that was supposed to be secure? I think the more quickly we move, the better off we'll be."

"Concur," Red agreed succinctly.

The three huddled close as they walked. Jay kept her head down, using her peripheral vision to see what was going on.

"I don't like this," she murmured.

"Me either, but we do the job and then we get paid," Rivka replied, soldiering forward through the throng of Pretarians.

"I get paid?" Jay asked.

"I suppose, but now you make me wonder. Damn! Do you get paid out of my pay—and I still have no idea what I'm getting paid—or do you get paid directly by the Federation, which seems unlikely at this point since they don't know I hired you unless Grainger did it for me. Follow?" Rivka looked back and forth as she walked. "Why don't these people believe in signs?"

"They know where they're going," Red answered. "It's just one more way to show their superiority over aliens and visitors."

"I have to admit that I'm beginning to share your low opinion of our hosts." Rivka looked down side tunnels as they passed. "Hospital?" she asked loudly.

She watched a couple heads look in the same direction. Without pause, she turned that way. Red followed, shaking his head.

"I'm not liking our chances in getting out of here." Red watched the Pretarians gather in the humans' wake.

"Then we'll go a different way," Rivka suggested, dismissing his concern.

"I'm not liking our chances of finding a different way out of here."

Jay chuckled, which made Rivka smile.

"Do you smell that?" Rivka asked. Red shook his head.

"I do," Jay replied. "Smells like the area where they brought the injured."

"Exactly. Follow that smell, Beauregard!" Rivka pointed forward.

"Who's Beauregard?" Red wondered.

"My favorite bloodhound." Rivka strode past a door and then stopped. She came back to it. She and Jay sniffed at it. "This is it."

"I'm not liking this at all," Red muttered as he pulled his shotgun from inside his coat. "This better be it, or we're fucked."

A mob of Pretarians was lining up behind them. Rivka opened the door and jumped inside, and Jay dove in right after her. Rivka reached back and pulled Red in. The door closed and they collectively breathed a sigh of relief, which ended when they turned around.

"I'm a Federation Magistrate!" Rivka declared from within the room, which appeared to be carved from the living rock. Red stood in front of the door, ready for it to open. Jay sat on the floor with her arms crossed.

"You told them that in the hospital. I think those were your last words when they hit us with the barrage of stun bolts. It impressed them then as much as it appears to now," Red deadpanned.

"They took my datapad."

Red turned around. "I feel for you." He had been stripped to his underwear and stood there in his boxers. Jay started to laugh while trying not to get caught looking at Red's body. "It's hot as fuck down here. Up here? I don't know where we are."

"I'll take the blame," Rivka told them softly. "They can't possibly think they are going to get away with this. Can they?"

Red turned back to the door and shrugged.

Jay hung her head between her knees and tried to think cool thoughts.

"They are going to kill us," Red suggested. He sat down next to Jay, sweat running from him. Rivka alone was tolerating the heat. Jay was flushed.

"Grainger, I wish I had accepted your offer of help," Rivka said. She checked on her two friends, then took off her shirt and started to fan them. Red leaned back and let the hot air evaporate the sweat, providing a brief respite. "I want my jacket."

"You'll get what they let you have," Red muttered.

"Do you have any secret lock-picking skills?" Rivka asked.

Jay shook her head. "Not that I know of."

"When we get out of here, what do you say we take a quick trip to Keome? I wonder if they hate the Pretarians as much as the Pretarians hate them." Rivka sighed.

"That's usually the case. It's hard to like someone who hates you," Jay added.

"I feel like shit," Red offered. He leaned to the side and puked. He straightened up before wiping his mouth on the back of his hairy arm. "There we go. Heat exhaustion, round forty-four."

"Heat ex becomes heat stroke, then you die," Rivka said matter-of-factly.

The door to the cell opened. Two guards stepped in, aiming their weapons at the humans.

"Really?" Rivka stated.

Sinraloo appeared behind the two. "It's good to see that you are still with us. Humans are so frail. I am surprised you survived the explosion. Not my bomb, by the way."

Rivka leaned toward the Pretarian, but the guards kept her from getting too close.

"Let me touch you," she offered. "I can tell just by touch whether you are telling the truth or not. You don't have to, but if you do, I can turn my investigation in a different direction. There's nothing more important than finding the bomber."

"You think you are still investigating a crime. How quaint!" Sinraloo backed into the corridor. "You are to return to your ship and leave Pretaria immediately."

Rivka wanted to bite the alien's head off, but the look of Red and Jay on the floor gave her the obvious answer. "We will. Please show us the way. I'll need my datapad and jacket. Red will need his clothes."

"I'm sorry. After your run-in with the vagrants when you were saved by our illustrious security force, none of the things you describe were with you. They brought you here for your security. You should thank them."

"My apologies, Sinraloo." Rivka choked back the snark that was ready to erupt. She had no choice but to hold back. She pulled Jay to her feet, then Red. The women each took an arm to help him walk. With one guard in the lead and one behind, they embarked on the longest and most painful walk of their lives.

When they finally arrived at the entrance, Jay was staggering and incoherent. Red was unconscious and balanced across Rivka's shoulders. The guard opened the door to let the heat waft in. "Do yourself a favor and rescind that treaty before you leave our system." Sinraloo turned and walked away.

"You missed your calling," Rivka said.

He stopped. "How so?"

"The job of Instigator pays good money on prison worlds. Maybe I can find you a spot." Rivka grabbed Jay's arm with her free hand and lumbered toward the ship. The hatch opened as she approached and she hurried toward it, using all she had left to get inside and button up the ship. She deposited the two in the lounge area and drew them large glasses of water. Jay could drink. She had to lean Red back and pour it down his throat.

She found the ship's medical kit. "Chaz, I need to hook Red up to an IV. Show me how to do that."

A video started to play, showing each step of the process. She followed along, cleaning the spot on his arm. With his low body fat and dehydration, his veins were almost bursting through his skin. She found the one she wanted, lined up the needle, and shoved it in. She taped it onto his arm as she hung the IV bag above the unconscious man. "That's twice now, Red. Who is whose bodyguard?"

"Chaz, get me Grainger."

After a short delay, a sleepy voice answered. "Nethers. You need a clock on that ship of yours."

"They threw us in jail and took all our stuff," she told him without preamble.

"You're not in jail now, I suppose, unless those folks have mastered the interstellar communication system, which they haven't. What did you do?"

"I tried to investigate the bombing."

"Do or do not, there is no try," Grainger mumbled.

"Nice reference. This planet hates the Keome with every fiber of their being, and now they hate humans, too. You're welcome."

"Did you lose your Magistrate's jacket?"

"Yes, they took that while I was unconscious."

"I would have razzed you about it, but that's not how you treat one of my Magistrates. I'm on my way."

"Why?" she asked.

"Because." He sounded more alert.

"I have not lost *all* control of this situation," Rivka countered.

"I'm glad you caveated that. I was wondering if you'd lost most of your dignity, or all of it. Thanks for clarifying."

"Don't be an ass," Rivka shot back. "This planet is home to the most hostile species I've ever met. Their idea of a treaty is they tell Keome they are assholes and the Keome agree and beg forgiveness. That's it. They have zero business sense. They are fueled by rage."

"Do you know who did it? Who bombed the meeting?" Grainger asked.

"No. I'd like to think it was Sinraloo and his cronies, but I'm not so sure anymore. I think it may have been the Keome, but I couldn't get close to them or Yutta, especially following the blast. I had issues with him from Day One. I wouldn't put it past him to have sabotaged the process by killing one of his own. I need to touch these guys, and it figures that they are allergic to physical contact or some such bullshit."

"You tried to touch them?"

"Of course."

"Like, with your arms out, staggering toward them, groaning for *brains?*"

"What?"

Grainger started to laugh and kept going. "Oh, God! Oh, Nethers, you're killing me, but you are 'Nethers' no more. Ha!"

"What in the holy fuck are you talking about?"

"Zombie. You are now Zombie. After Jael hears this story, you will be known as nothing else."

"And I thought the heat melted my brain. You are a total cross-eyed glory-hole whale-wiper."

"Nice try, Zombie. Back to business, since you're cutting into my beauty sleep and you know how much I need that. When it comes to your case, you don't know anything?"

"Not a damn thing. They were holding Yus' family hostage. Once he agreed to sign the treaty, their lives were forfeit. Maybe he suicided as a way out."

"Those are quite the range of theories. Why are you calling me?"

"The heat nearly killed Red and Jay, and I've been kicked off the planet. We're taking a short trip to Keome to see what they think about all this, then I'm coming back here to set things right."

"You mean mete out Justice."

"Exactly."

"So you don't need anything from me except comic relief?"

"Exactly. First beer is on me."

"I think the first beer will always be on you. I'm calling it right now. Grainger out."

"Wait!" she said, but it was too late.

She prepared a second bag for Red's IV. "Chaz, take us to Keome, please. Best possible speed."

"The Pretarians have not granted us clearance to depart. I have requested it, but they inform me it will be a few hours before we can go."

"Is there a safety reason why we can't, like a meteor shower or something?"

"Nothing that I can detect."

"Take off, on my authority. Ignore the Pretarians. They don't get to detain a Magistrate, not a second time in one day, anyway. Bring weapons online, activate the gravitic shields, and prepare to fire."

"On whom should I fire?"

"Any Pretarian ship that tries to stop us."

"As you wish, Magistrate. Lifting off. Next stop, Keome."

The ship lifted away from the planet and arced into the sky.

"Anything?" Rivka asked.

"Clear space ahead, Magistrate."

"At least they had the common decency for something."

The ship rocked and juked. "Beginning evasive maneuvers. Ground fire. An ion cannon's energy bolts are bracketing us. Leaving the atmosphere. We are in space.

Preparing to Gate across the system. Gate is formed. Entering the Gate. We are over Keome."

"Damn, that is what efficiency looks like. Thank you, Chaz. That ground fire wasn't close, was it?"

"Not in the least, Magistrate," the EI responded.

"Outside temperature?" Rivka asked.

"Cooler than Pretaria by four degrees," Chaz answered.

"A cold spell. How will we manage?" Rivka shook her head. "What the hell is up with these planets? Chaz, I promise you that I will check ambient temperatures before I accept my next case. This blast-furnace climate is intolerable. No wonder they don't have wildlife! I'm surprised *any* life evolved here."

"A welcoming committee is outside the ship, Magistrate."

"All ashore who's going ashore!" Rivka called. Red was on his second bag of saline and barely conscious. Jay was slumped in a chair, rhythmically stroking Hamlet. "When that bag is done, give him a third one. Our big boy is thirsty. I won't be gone long."

Jay didn't have enough energy to argue.

"Close and lock the door after me, Chaz," Rivka called as she headed into the heat. It was every bit as oppressive here, maybe more so because of the humidity. Rivka did her best not to make faces.

She approached the tall multi-armed aliens. "I'm Magistrate Rivka Anoa. I'm pleased to meet you," she began, with little enthusiasm.

One of the Keome stepped forward. "We appreciate your efforts to save the lives of our delegation to accursed Pretaria."

Here we go, Rivka thought.

"But we must condemn your arbitrated treaty in the strongest terms."

"Do you know how your people are doing? When will they return to Keome?"

"When they are able to travel; maybe a few more days. Thank you for asking. Now, let's talk about this ill-advised treaty."

Let's not and say we did, she thought. "What rankles you the most about it?"

"It treats Keome and Pretaria as equals, and we most assuredly are not!"

Rivka breathed slowly, happy to find that the Keome didn't get under her skin. "What does Federation law say on this issue? Because disputes between two planets who are both in the Federation surrender to the superior law—Federation law—to which Keome and Pretaria are both signatories." She smiled pleasantly before raising her voice. "What does the law say?"

"I'm sure I don't know!"

"Then find out, because the treaty was arbitrated according to Federation law. That happens when you request arbitration, which Keome and Pretaria did. There is nothing further to discuss. If you would like to challenge the arbitrated treaty, you can do that. The process is contained in the Federation's Law of Arbitration, the penultimate section. Good luck with that. Now, I have some questions regarding the attack on the delegations. I'd like a private place to conduct my interviews, and I expect to start seeing your people in about fifteen minutes."

The welcoming committee's spokesman looked like he no longer wanted to speak for the group. Another stepped up. "Of course. Please come this way."

"I'm sorry. I need to contact my ship." The Keome pointed to the corvette, parked immediately behind her. She ignored him. "Chaz, I need you to stay in constant contact with me. If you lose contact, start destroying this planet and continue blowing things up until contact is restored."

She turned back to her hosts. "Shall we?" Rivka motioned for them to precede her.

"Wait!" the original spokesman exclaimed. "What was that for?"

"On Pretaria, I failed to install a safety protocol, and I was blown up, attacked, robbed, and jailed. I will now implement that order whenever I meet with anyone in the Intripas system. People who hate aren't to be trusted, because their emotions override their reasoning. If you aren't like Pretaria, you have nothing to worry about. Shall we?"

One of the aliens stepped away from the group and hurried into the nearest building. Unlike Pretaria, most of the Keome structures were aboveground. They were low, but extended in both directions for as far as Rivka could see.

She started to follow the alien who left, but the rest of the group waved at her to go with them. The angled toward a different building.

"Where did he go?" Rivka asked the first spokesman. He

didn't reply. "Makes me think the Keome were planning something untoward. It pains me to see subterfuge. A very smart person told me that everyone lies, and I have found that to be true. What mistruths are you going to tell me?"

The alien continued to look forward, actively ignoring her questions. She looked to the others, and no one would meet her gaze.

"No matter. I will find out, the crimes will be tallied, and the guilty punished."

19

"Where's Rivka?" Red mumbled as he came to. He shivered, and it felt good. He was in the ship's mess deck, the lounge, the rec room; all the things they called the corvette's communal space. "What the hell?" He noticed the IV. "Not again..."

"Yup, again. Rivka is with the Keome."

"I have to get out there."

"Nope. She said to stay here, plus I can't see where she's gone, but Chaz is in constant contact with her. She gave some weird order that if we lost contact with her, the ship was to destroy the planet."

"Can it do that?" Red asked skeptically as he yanked out the IV and held a finger on the puncture wound.

"Hey!" Jay slapped at his hand to take a look, then she carefully took the needle, tube, and bag and dumped it into the recycler. "I don't think it can. I suppose it was a bluff because the Keome seemed to be as friendly as the Pretarians."

"Are we on Keome?" It finally dawned on Red that they'd left Pretaria.

"Right again. Rivka said the climate was worse here. A few degrees cooler, but the humidity makes it stifling. She didn't say it, but I will. You wouldn't last thirty seconds out there. Me neither."

"Is that your attempt at cheering me up?"

"Did it work?"

"Not really," Red told her.

"Then no. I'm not sure what we're supposed to do while she's gone. She didn't say."

"You said Chaz is in constant contact with her." Red stood on unsteady legs, stretched, and continued to the bridge. "Chaz, I want to listen in on the Magistrate. Please pipe the feed to the speaker."

"I believe there is a privacy clause that comes into play here: attorney/client privilege," the EI responded.

"But they aren't her clients. They are all suspects in an ongoing investigation, unless she's doing something different. And still, they wouldn't be *her* clients. Regardless, I'm her bodyguard, and I'm in here and not out there protecting her. If something happens, I'll hear it and be able to respond."

"You will now be able to listen. Please inform me if you wish to speak to her, since our microphone is muted."

"Thanks, Chaz. You're one of the team."

"Is this a compliment?" the EI asked.

"It is, now stay quiet. I can't hear what's going on." Red leaned back in the captain's chair and closed his eyes to focus his attention.

Rivka walked into the building, immediately thankful that an air conditioning system was functioning to remove most of the humidity and some of the temperature. Still nearly as hot as a cup of coffee, but it was a reprieve.

The room to which they led her was empty, without a table or chairs or decoration of any sort. It was little more than a closet.

"Here is a room you can use for your *interviews*," the Keome said, dragging out the last word.

"Thank you. The first interviewee will be the chairman of the welcoming committee, which would be you. The next will be Yus' spouse. I need information that only she has. After I talk with her, I will give you the remainder of the names. There shouldn't be more than three or four, I suspect.

"But I had nothing to do with anything. I happened to be close when we received the call that a human had arrived..."

Rivka interrupted him. "Thank you for the information, but I'd like to start the interview. The others can go." She shooed them away and closed the door, leaving her alone with her surprised guest.

"I have nothing to say," the Keome told her.

"That sounded like something." Rivka reached toward the alien and stopped when she recalled Grainger's near-hysterical laughter. Zombie. She shook her head and kept approaching the alien.

"What are you doing?"

"Sounds like you have plenty to say, for someone who

has nothing to say." She trapped him in the corner and he held his four hands in front of him, but she parried the defense and grabbed him by one wrist.

Horror! Getting touched by a Pretarian-lover. Hide the truth. They had worked with the Pretarians to torpedo the treaty. The hated Pretarians! But they had agreed on one thing—they couldn't work together. Villains and scum!

Rivka stepped back. "You have got to be shitting me! Does that make any sense at all?"

"I don't know what you mean," the Keome muttered weakly as he rubbed the spot Rivka had touched on his arm .

"You worked with the Pretarians to prove that you couldn't work with the Pretarians. They expelled me from their planet, yet you call me a Pretarian-lover. I'll let you in on a little secret: I'm a Federation lover. A Magistrate in love with the law. The treaty, dutifully and legally enacted as part of a lawful request for arbitration, will remain in effect and be enforced by our considerable Federation assets. In other words, it sucks to be you."

"I didn't say a word!" the Keome shouted.

"I don't need you to say anything, and it helps if you don't. You're kind of a jerk, and it's painful enough to see the bigotry in your mind. I don't want it slamming into my eardrums too."

"But I didn't say a word!"

"You said a *shitload* of words, most of them stupid and some of them demonstrating your complicity in a crime—the terroristic act of bombing the delegation, which leads to a second charge of murder. Since you and your cronies used a bomb, that falls under the reckless disregard for life standard, which makes it a capital crime. Do you understand the charges as I've stated them?"

"What? What is this? I am Governor Prikasor, and I will not participate in this charade!"

He tried to push past her, but Rivka was first to the door and blocked his way. "With four arms, you guys must be hellacious at Charades," she remarked, leaning back, putting a foot against the door, and crossing her arms.

"No!" he wailed.

"Capital murder." She glared at him. His veneer started to crack as he contemplated his role in the affair.

"No," he whispered.

"Capital murder." Rivka held her pose. "You do understand that I can carry out sentencing right now. You could have seconds to live."

The governor sat on the floor so he could bury his head in his hands. "What do you want?" he mumbled between his fingers.

Yus' wife was elderly. She limped into the ad hoc interview room looking for a chair, and was disappointed to not find one. Rivka leaned into the corridor where the governor faced the wall, shaking. "Hey! Get her a chair, and be quick about it." The governor waved at someone beyond him.

Rivka went back into the room. "I'm so sorry for your loss, ma'am," Rivka started. She'd never had to have *the* talk with anyone before. "I worked with Yus for only a short time, but found him to be a Keome of honor. He had a vision for the future that doesn't seem to be popular—one where the Keome and the Pretarians work together. He knew what had to be done, and did it. The new treaty? He drafted that, in conjunction with Maseer, the Pretarian delegate. I believe they became friends."

"I told him it would get us killed, but I thought they'd want to make him watch as they tortured me. I expect they still will do something to me. The people are very angry."

"Help me to understand, because I don't. I don't know why the Keome would rather shrivel up and die than engage in a joint trade deal with your sister planet."

"And that is where you err. Not our sister planet, but a cast-off; the refuse of what we were. We have nothing in common with them." The door opened slowly and someone slid a chair in. Rivka hurried to move it closer to the elder.

"The only thing you have in common is everything. You descend from a common ancestor, and most importantly, today you are both in a state of decline. If something isn't done, both of your races will die. You would die for your hatred?"

"Everything dies," she said glumly.

"An idea can live forever." Rivka leaned over the woman, brushing her hand against the back of the elder's arm.

Sadness. And hope.

"I promise you that I will find who did this, so we can show two worlds that there is a better way. The way of Yus and Maseer."

The Keome didn't nod their heads, but the old woman raised hers and smiled. "I trust you, human, as my husband said he would trust you."

"Who do I need to talk with to root out the truth? Who would know? Tell me, and I will have them brought here."

"I cannot. My husband protected me by making sure I knew nothing of those who opposed him."

"But they can't risk it. They'll assume you know. You have no leverage over them. I'm sorry." Rivka ducked her head as she tried to think. "You have to know a name to get me started. I'm pretty good at getting information."

"Klobis," she whispered.

Rivka leaned toward the older Keome. "I'll take care of it. For your husband and for all Keome, I'll get to the bottom of it."

She helped the woman to her feet, and they walked out together.

She watched the elder shuffle away before finding the governor. He tried to turn away, but she caught one of his arms. She pulled him down to her. "Bring me Klobis," she growled.

"Whatcha listening to?" Jay asked, entering the bridge carrying Hamlet.

"The Magistrate. She asks questions and they don't answer, but she hears them anyway. Is she a telepath?" Red scrubbed at the start of a beard. He needed to shave.

Jay shrugged. "Does it matter?"

"I guess not, but I don't like the thought of other people in my head. I think weird shit."

"And sex, I suspect."

"I'm a guy," Red replied.

"Are you going to put some clothes on?"

Red looked at himself, realizing that he was still in his boxers. "I'll be damned. Where are my clothes?"

"Really? You went this whole time and never realized that you are parading around the ship in your underwear?"

"I've been preoccupied. My client is out there, and I'm not protecting her. The least I can do is listen and try to be comfortable that she's not in danger when I know that she is."

"How do you know that?"

"Because." Red wanted to leave it at that, but decided that Jay deserved more of an explanation. "Despite the extra arms and eyeballs, these people are just like the Pretarians. They can't be trusted."

"Tell me something I don't know."

"If you tickle a wombat they will laugh."

Jay opened her mouth as if to reply. Red laughed until he heard Rivka start to talk, then held a finger over his lips and leaned closer to the speaker.

"Klobis," she said dryly. The alien was huge. Not tall, but wide, in contrast to the other Keome Rivka had met. His was a decadent life, one that didn't require manual labor of any sort. Add that to eating too well, and the result was Klobis.

"I heard Yus' bag suggested you talk with me."

"Yus' bag? Is there no end to your putrescence?" she asked.

"Since you have to ask, no. Why am I here?" the alien

asked, trying to loom over the puny human. Rivka stood her ground.

Just a little bit closer. "Why did you coordinate with the Pretarians?" she asked and grabbed him by his closest arm. She leaned forward, expecting him to pull away, but he pushed toward her instead.

Power. Control. Leader of a world in decline was better than having a good life and being no one.

She staggered backward as he sought to pin her against the wall, then twisted sideways, using her small size to dodge him and then used her immense strength to throw him face-first into that very wall. She twisted one of his arms behind him while trying to kick his legs apart, but Klobis wouldn't budge.

The huge Keome used his other three arms to push himself clear. Feeling herself falling, she lashed out, driving the toe of her boot between his legs. She connected, and the fight ended with the Keome curled on the floor, whimpering. Rivka rolled him over and grabbed him by the ears to stare into the eyes on the back of his head.

"I know why, but how did you do it?"

Leverage. Threaten the families. Hostages. Luxuries. Sometimes both.

"Who planted the bomb?"

An image of Yutta jumped into Klobis' mind. A willing martyr. He wanted nothing more than to keep Keome from falling under Pretarian power. Klobis handing over the components of the bomb. Klobis giving the order. Klobis talking with Sinraloo, plotting a backup in case Yutta failed.

"Don't you understand? Neither of you has *anything*.

Both of your planets are poor, and your people suffering. The treaty will change all that. You are fighting to be the king of the anthill while the throne on the mountaintop stays empty. You could have climbed something that mattered, but you chose to wallow in the cesspool of your own filth. Klobis, I, Magistrate Rivka Anoa have found you guilty of terrorism, conspiracy to commit murder, multiple counts of attempted murder, and the murder of Yus. Your plea is irrelevant. I sentence you to death for crimes against your people."

"*Wait*," the Keome cried, before finding his last vestiges of strength and shouting, "*I SAID WAIT!*"

Rivka reached around his head and tucked her elbows close to her body as she pushed and pulled while driving upward with her legs. The Keome's neck snapped with surprising ease, and she almost fell over.

"Justice is served," she panted.

Her chest heaved, not from the effort, but from the power of the emotions flooding through her. She slowed her breathing, straightened her shirt, and opened the door.

Rivka motioned for the governor. "You have been manipulated your whole time in power by people like him. It's time to think for yourself. The Pretarians are not your enemy, only creatures like Klobis. Clean up that mess in there, or not. It's your call. My job here is finished."

The Magistrate forced her way through the crowded hallway and outside into the heat. "Chaz, fire up the ship. We're going back to Pretaria."

20

"Where in the hell did those ships come from?" Rivka demanded.

"I don't know, but they are interfering with our ability to Gate. Our gravitic shields are in place."

"Are they going to fire on us?" Jay asked in alarm. She started to tremble.

"It's okay. Dying in space is quick and easy, so there's nothing to worry about."

"Holy shit, Red! Is that your idea of being comforting?" Rivka risked a quick glance over her shoulder before returning her attention to the main screen. "Open a comm channel, Chaz."

"Channel open," the EI reported.

"My fellow spaceships," Rivka started, hesitant to call them enemy or friend or anything that would grant them legal status. She was confusing herself. Red groaned. "We interpret your activities as a prelude to attack. Please cease your emissions immediately."

The Magistrate waited. "They're not answering."

"The channel is open, but I can't be sure they received the message," the EI replied.

Rivka swallowed and pursed her lips. "Repeat the message and send a call for help to the Bad Company just in case."

Jay cried out and ran from the bridge.

"Not everyone takes their impending doom well," Red suggested before he took another bite from one of the noxious protein bars he found so appealing.

"Can you tell if these are Keome, or Pretarian, or something else completely?"

"Those are Keome vessels, and if my records are complete, they represent the entire Keome fleet. The interference has ceased."

An image appeared on the screen. Four arms and chameleon-like skin—a Keome. "We had a request from Keome to detain you for questioning."

"Who did the request come from?"

"Governor Prikasor."

"Please connect me to the governor, if you would be so kind." Rivka smiled at the screen. The Keome considered the request before waving one of his arms at someone behind him. With eyes in the back of his head, he didn't need to turn to face them.

The image was instantly replaced by a new one. The governor looked at her.

"You have a lot to answer for!" he shouted.

"I do, but not to you. I have conducted myself in accordance with Federation law, which are the rules that guide my actions. Do you want me to come back down there?

Because if I do, I'll be charging you with conspiracy? I know you were in Klobis' pocket."

"I was not!" he denied adamantly.

She had been bluffing. His response led her to believe that *he* wasn't associated with Klobis, but someone above him had been.

"Who do you answer to?" she asked.

"The Keome in the capital province. I answer to them every two years when they vote."

"Klobis was guilty as sin. Defending him doesn't make you an associate, but it does make me wonder about your understanding of what's going on under your nose."

The image appeared to freeze as the governor assumed a statue's pose.

"Who are your advisors—the ones who tell you what is going on, and where to focus your energy?" Rivka asked. *No one is giving orders, but they are manipulating him nonetheless.*

"You have been cleared to leave and good riddance," the governor finally managed before cutting the link. Space appeared where his image had been.

Rivka wanted to do something about the governor, but wasn't sure what. Incompetence wasn't a crime. "Chaz, take us back to Pretaria."

The corvette slammed into the upper atmosphere, shields glowing as Chaz forced the ship downward.

Red had finally dressed. He was carrying one of the two

Pretarian guards' weapons. Jay carried the other. "You two think you're going along?"

"Of course. I hear the third time's a charm. I've never had a woman carry me back to her house before, let alone three times. It's like the holy trinity for a man."

Rivka looked down her nose at him. "Next time I'm going to leave your big ass on the ground. Maybe think about eating a salad every now and then."

"What are you talking about? This is Grade-A prime bistok." He gave her his most winning smile.

"You're miffed because these are aliens and you can't win them over with a smile and a toss of your silken locks."

"I'm miffed because it's like the hellfires of Hades out there, and in here we got a cat. Everywhere I turn the universe has conspired against me."

"Only one of us returned to the ship in our underwear."

"I'm never going to live that down, am I?"

"Probably not. Are you people ready? Sinraloo and Yutta are the conspirators. Yutta pulled the trigger, but Sinraloo was the backup plan. They are both going to answer to me."

The flight smoothed once the ship made it through the upper atmosphere, but Chaz continued his steep descent. The ion cannons fired again, this time much closer.

"Return fire, Chaz. Take out that cannon."

Two missiles popped out of their canisters on the top of the ship, fired their gravitic thrusters, and raced away from the ship. Their engines kicked in, and they accelerated downward. Even without a warhead, a ballistic projectile traveling at hypersonic speed would do a great deal of damage to a weapon as delicate as an ion cannon.

In moments, the firing had stopped. The corvette raced downward, pulling up at the last second and landing in the same spot they had been before. The door opened, and stairs descended while the ship was still settling. Rivka stormed off, followed closely by Red and Jay.

She rammed through the doors and was surprised to find the entry empty. "Chaz, contact the Pretarians and tell them I'm waiting for Maseer."

"He is still in the hospital. It was barely a day ago that he was severely injured."

"It's been less than a day?" Rivka replied, turning to Jayita and Vered. She finally noticed how tired they looked. "When is the last time I slept?"

"It has been thirty-eight hours, Magistrate," the EI replied, no concern in his voice.

"I'll be damned."

"Maseer has agreed to come," Chaz added. "It will take him a while since he'll be in a wheelchair."

"I need all of the members of the delegation."

"Stand by."

"There is a direct elevator to the hospital. I can fly you there," Chaz offered after communing with the Pretarians.

"Back to the ship," Rivka ordered. "And tell them we'll be there shortly. No one goes anywhere. And tell them to bring our stuff. I want my fucking jacket."

Rivka kicked the door open as she led the way back to the ship. When they boarded, she found Red sweating heavily.

"You are on the sidelines for the rest of this mission."

"I'll be fine," he tried to argue.

"I'm calling bullshit! The bullshit lever has been pulled.

Show Jay how to work that thing, because you're staying here." Rivka waved at the weapon.

"But..."

Rivka closed with her bodyguard. "You know I'm right. In your condition, you're a liability. We'll get you fixed up with the Pod-doc when we get back, but for now, you need to stay here. I think the next planet we go to will approach absolute zero."

"I'm good with cold."

"Compared to here? I think I'll take cold, too," Jay agreed.

"Prepare for landing," Chaz told them.

"Same rule as last time, Red. If we drop out of contact, start blowing shit up until we get back in touch. Chaz, do as Red tells you."

"Roger." Red wasn't feeling great about being left behind. What made it worse was that he knew Rivka was right. He'd never been a liability before.

"I'm not sure I like that rule," the EI replied.

"You don't *like* something? How very AI of you. I don't *want* you to start laying waste to the planet, but sometimes, people need to be put in their places. Arresting a Magistrate? No. Hell no, and fuck no. That was a dumbass move that they will pay for."

The hatch opened and steps extended to the ground. Rivka and Jay followed them down. A single Pretarian waited at a lone entrance to the building. He used a key and went inside. Without a word, the three climbed aboard the elevator. It took them down farther than Rivka remembered going.

"Chaz?"

"Your signal is growing weak, Magistrate. Shall I start blowing shit up, as you put it?"

"Not yet. Wait for Red to give you the order."

Jay raised one eyebrow.

"Blond looks good on you," Rivka told her.

"And you, too. I do like mine longer, but this heat is making me reconsider. Next time, if you have any influence over the process, pick a tropical paradise instead of the surface of the sun."

"We'll wrap this up soon and go back to the house. I need a shower, as much from my own sweat as the hatred that leaves a bad smell on everything."

The elevator stopped, and the doors opened. The Pretarian waited, allowing the humans to go out first. "Oh, no," Rivka told him. "You go first. I don't trust your people. Please don't take it personally."

When the Pretarian left the elevator, the corridor was empty. He walked to a door, opened it, and went inside. Rivka hurried after him. When she peeked inside, she found that they were at a back entrance to the hospital. She waved for Jay to follow. She saw who she was looking for.

The hospital was a wide-open area separated by equipment and a few curtains. The area for the Keome was clearly separate from the Pretarians. That was where Rivka was going. Yutta was standing outside the curtains.

Rivka shot across the hospital floor, never taking her eyes from the Keome. Pretarians tried to intercept her, but she wasn't having it. She pushed them out of the way as she brazenly plowed ahead. Yutta backed into the area and disappeared behind a curtain, and Rivka started to run.

She signaled for Jay to go wide and block him from

escaping. Rivka ripped the curtain aside as she crouched, ready to be attacked.

Yutta stood there holding all four hands out. *Stop.*

"You have no place here, human," he told her. Miento was on a gurney with her eyes closed, but her chest moved slowly. An IV was hooked to one of her arms. The others, Suarpok and Ome, were in their beds, but looked at Rivka with alert eyes.

"You have no place *anywhere*, Yutta. I, Magistrate Rivka Anoa, have found you guilty of terrorism, conspiracy to commit murder, attempted murder, and the murder of Yus."

Miento's eyes fluttered open. "What?" she asked weakly.

"I'm sure I don't know what she's talking about. You know humans. They make stuff up, just like that treaty. A complete fabrication. A Federation lie."

"You received your direction and the bomb from Klobis. We have his testimony on record. We have already adjudicated his case."

Yutta turned to the others, who were no longer looking at Rivka.

"You killed Yus?" Miento mumbled. She tried to sit up, but the pain was too great. "You were willing to kill all of us, too?"

"Wait!" Yutta cried.

"Interesting," Rivka mused. "That was Klobis' last word."

Yutta looked around rapidly. He'd boxed himself in. "Federation lies!" He pointed a long finger at Rivka. "*She's* the enemy. The Federation is our enemy."

"The Keome and the Pretarians have more in common

than we let ourselves see," Maseer said from a wheelchair behind Rivka.

Rivka stepped back where she could see Maseer and Yutta. "Sinraloo and Yutta were partners, as bizarre as that sounds. They worked together to show that they couldn't work together. I can't fathom their logic."

Yutta jumped, trying to get over the wheelchair to run for freedom. Rivka let him go. Where could a Keome hide on Pretaria?

It didn't matter, since he was blocked from leaving the hospital. Pretarian guards closed in from all sides and he went down under a barrage of stun weapons, the type that Rivka, Jay, and Red had been subjected to.

"How are you feeling, Maseer?" Rivka asked.

"Betrayed," he shared. "I don't know why Sinraloo would be involved."

Rivka shrugged. "When we find him, we'll ask."

"He's not here, but this is Pretaria. He won't be able to hide for long."

"Assuming he's in hiding." Rivka waved to the others from the Pretarian delegation. The three joined Maseer. "If you haven't been told, the treaty has been transmitted and is in place. Did any of you have a chance to read it before Yutta and Sinraloo's subterfuge?"

"The main guarantee in the treaty is that a percentage of your people will have the opportunity to work out in the galaxy. It is only a temporary solution until your two planets can establish viable exports. What you do have is people who can work in extreme heat. The main point of law is about the importation of labor. The Federation guarantees work visas across all its planets. You will be advised by an immigration delegation that I've already requested."

"The treaty simply gives both people the right to self-determination; that their future is theirs to shape. What is wrong with that?" Maseer intoned. He held his chest after he spoke. Beneath his hospital gown were wounds beyond the physical.

A small commotion at the door drew Rivka's attention.

"Sinraloo!" she yelled and started to run, dodging around Pretarians and equipment alike. Sinraloo casually stepped back through the door. Rivka screamed her fury.

"Follow the traitor!" Maseer called as loudly as he could manage.

A guard reached for Rivka, and she punched him in the face without slowing down.

"Not her, you idiot! It's Sinraloo!"

Rivka burst into the corridor and saw Sinraloo running in the direction of the train platform. She accelerated, using all the power of her enhancements to propel her forward. She heard the guards behind her, but they couldn't keep up. She danced left and right as she ran, the Pretarians less than congenial in getting out of her way.

Sinraloo disappeared into a side room. She rammed through the door and was greeted by a length of pipe that caught her in the chest. She felt something break as her feet came out from under her. She flipped head over heels and landed on her face. Someone jumped on her back and slammed her face into the floor.

"The universe will forget you ever existed," Sinraloo snarled from behind her.

Rivka pushed up and twisted. A bolt of pain shot through her chest, but the weight fell from her back. She launched herself forward and rolled. More searing pain. She popped upright and balanced on the balls of her feet as she tried to figure out a way to fight her enemy.

Sinraloo picked up the pipe, which was the length of a baseball bat. He wound up to swing and Rivka backed up, her eyes darting at the stuff around her. Improvised weapons. There was nothing sharp. There was nothing easy to throw. Rounded desks without chairs. It looked like a storeroom without much stuff in it.

"I need your pipe so I can beat you with it," she told him.

"I think I'll hang on to it a little while longer," he replied. "Listen! Do you hear that?"

Rivka continued to adjust until she had a desk between her and Sinraloo.

"It's the sound of the guards running by. They aren't selected for their intelligence, but they serve a purpose—just not for you."

"I'll have my coat back, too. You can keep the datapad. You can't access it, so fuck you."

"Is that the best you have, Magistrate?" He sneered, then feinted one way, swung, dodged and swung again. Rivka leaned forward, and he lunged. She slapped the pipe down and powered through a right cross that exploded Sinraloo's nose. As he started to fall, she grabbed the pipe and leapt to the side.

She gripped it in two hands and swung overhead,

bringing it down like an axe on the back of his head. Sinraloo collapsed on the desk, his skull crushed.

"You're not coming back from that one." Rivka spoke one word with each breath. "You have been judged and found wanting."

She tossed the pipe on his back, but it rolled off and clattered to the floor. She walked slowly to the door, stopped, and turned.

"Justice is served," she whispered before entering the corridor and walking back to the hospital, nodding and greeting the Pretarians as if they were old friends.

They didn't respond in kind. *Someday you'll thank me, but today is not that day.*

21

"I can't thank you enough, Maseer, for your support of the process," Rivka said, offering her hand before quickly pulling it back. "Sorry, shaking hands is a human thing to do."

"Human physiology may not be best suited for our planet, but your psychology is just what we need. *I* thank *you*, Magistrate."

"I am not going to miss the heat, but I am going to miss you, my friend," Rivka told him with a smile.

Jay nodded her agreement.

"At your request, Yutta is being transferred to Keome custody. We would be more than happy to deal with him if you need us to."

"No. You don't need new reasons for tension between your planets. You still have a long way to go."

Maseer watched the humans from his wheelchair. "I've asked the guards to search Sinraloo's office. We shall see what they find."

"Will they do it?"

"As you've seen, news travels fast on Pretaria. Sinraloo's complicity in the attack and his willingness to work with the Keome to discredit the arbitration is going to have the opposite effect from what he intended—it *adds* credibility to what we've done. I am sorry that Yus had to die and miss seeing the fruits of our efforts."

"Talking about missing..." Rivka started slowly. She held out her hand and Jay put a datapad into it. "I added a couple things before I transmitted the treaty. The first bit here," she pointed to the screen as she held it where Maseer could see it, "is about equal medical care. It is amazing that Miento is still alive, but thank goodness. Pretarian doctors needed to treat her sooner. And then this last part. It came from a movie I like and think is hilarious. They aren't wrong."

"Be excellent to each other?" Maseer asked.

"It's what we barristers call 'precatory language.' It's nonbinding, but it is there nonetheless. There's no remedy if one is not excellent to another, but it is my desire. As you have been excellent to me, I hope that I have been excellent to you."

"You have. It has been quite some time since I had Turbid Pie." Maseer stopped. He hadn't just eaten a meal, he had shared it with a new friend—a friend who was now gone. "Damn. I understood Yus. I will miss him, and the conversations we would have had."

"I'll be here for a while," Miento croaked. Jay poured water into a glass on a side table. Miento drank the whole thing, cradling the glass in two hands while holding herself upright with the other two.

"Extra arms must be convenient," Maseer observed.

"It's all the fashion where I come from," Miento replied.

Jay and Rivka waited in the small room at the top of the elevator. The corvette was parked outside within spitting distance. A Pretarian guard stood with them, his expression neutral as he looked out the window. "What are we waiting for?" Rivka pressed.

"Maseer said to wait."

"If Yutta appears, I'll stuff him in the airlock and jettison his body when we reach space."

Jay looked sideways at the Magistrate.

"I'm kidding, but I'm ready to go. I think it's gotten hotter."

Jay tipped her chin toward the door.

"Go ahead. I'll catch up."

Jay bolted before Rivka could change her mind. The corvette's hatch opened, and Jay took the steps two at a time as she climbed inside. The hatch closed behind her.

"She's already enjoying the cool of the ship," Rivka said to no one in particular. The elevator door hissed open, and two guards walked out carrying the team's missing clothes and equipment. Despite the heat, the first thing Rivka reached for was her jacket. She put it on and traced the outline of the Federation's Magistrate emblem, a star holding the scales of Justice.

She held out her arms for everything else, and they piled it on. "Damn, Red! How much junk do you carry?"

"A lot. It takes a lot to protect a Magistrate. The galaxy's criminals may hate you, but they all want to *be* you," a voice told her from the datapad cradled in her arm.

"Talking about junk! Yours was all over my shoulder, and I need about ten more showers to get the stench off me."

The guard held the door, his neck beads clacking, and Rivka jogged for the climate-controlled wonderland of her corvette. The hatch opened, the stairs dropped, and she vaulted inside.

"Chaz! Take us home."

"I can't be last. Does it matter that I adjudicated *two* cases?" Rivka pleaded.

Grainger crossed his arms and shook his head.

"From the top of the mountain to the deepest valley she falls. But I got the law right, didn't I?"

"Sure, but any goofy fucker can get *that* part right. It's how you massage it into place without beating people over the head with it that will make you great."

"Then why do I train so hard to beat people over the head?"

"Because we're not perfect. We're Magistrates. Let me buy you a beer so we can tell lies in the peace and comfort of our drunken stupor."

"Are the others here?"

"Only Bustamove. He arrived about two minutes before you did, but that still makes you last."

"I think you suck," she told him. Red tried not to snicker and failed.

"Pod-doc for you, Lightweight, and Zombie, you come with me."

"I used to be 'Lightweight,' so treat my name well," Rivka called over her shoulder. Red followed them. Grainger stopped and turned to face Rivka's bodyguard.

"No, the Pod-doc is waiting for you. I'll watch over her—you have my word. You need to be ready since she could be called up any moment now. First order of business is to be ready to deploy. We can't have the Magistrate carrying you through a case again."

Red looked crushed until Grainger hammered him on the shoulder. The big man staggered, anger flashing across his face. "We get the nanocytes because they help us do our jobs better. They are just a tool that you need in your toolbox."

"I'll take that explanation. I'll be down as quickly as I can. I owe the Magistrate a beer."

They both watched Red walk away.

"He's good, isn't he?" Grainger asked.

"The best; committed and loyal. Why was he available?"

"He doesn't like working for scumbags. He left his last two employers high and dry because they were doing horrible things. They bought his protection, but they paid for his silence, too. He couldn't do it. The big man has a sense of honor. But those former employers put a hit on him. There's a permanent price on his head. He either works for us or disappears, possibly into the corona of a sun."

"I'll keep an eye out. I like him watching my back. It's one less thing to worry about. On a topic that is nearer and dearer to me, I think I did a good job out there."

"What do you want, approval from me? You have it. That case, just like almost every one we get, was tough. It could have been resolved a dozen different ways. Your way might not be my way, but in the end, all that matters is that you can defend it in a court of law."

"I can do that," she replied.

"Be excellent to each other?"

"You *did* read it." Rivka bobbed her head while biting her lip.

"There's Buster."

Rivka had already seen the Magistrate waving from inside the bar. They joined him. Two extra drinks were already sitting on the table. Rivka reached for one. Bustamove slammed his hand down. "What the fuck do you think you're doing?"

She was taken aback and stammered, "I was taking my drink."

"Get your own damn drink. These are mine."

"All three?"

"Didn't we tell you? Nanocytes keep you from getting drunk unless you overpower them."

"You *didn't* tell me that," Rivka countered. "How was the R2D2 case?"

"A lot of looking through really boring shit. You'd think I was back doing lawyer stuff. Read all this documentation and write us a paper! Yeah." Buster shook his head.

"You weren't a Ranger first?" Rivka asked.

Both Buster and Grainger put a finger to their lips. "We don't ever say that word," Grainger cautioned.

"Nope, I was a lawyer, but then I got a clue because the

system was letting way too many hard-core criminals loose. I found a different way."

"That comes across as more on the vigilante side of the legal spectrum and not the uphold-the-law side."

Buster fixed her with a hard stare, and she slid her hand to his untouched drink and threw it back before he could stop her.

"You owe me a Supernova," he told her evenly.

"And a beer. Bartender! A new round, on my tab," she called toward the bar.

"Now you're speaking my language." Buster gave her a thumbs-up.

Grainger's pad buzzed.

"We're on vacation," Buster said. "Don't answer it."

"It's Nathan Lowell. Do you want me to tell him that you told me not to take his call?" Grainger tapped the pad, and the president of the Bad Company appeared. "Hey, Nathan, what brings you to my neck of the woods?"

"That new Magistrate of yours committed the Bad Company to hire a bunch of tall aliens. What the hell am I supposed to do with a bunch of tall aliens?"

Grainger turned the pad to show Rivka. She waved timidly at the screen, her eyes wide in shock.

"There you are!" Nathan declared.

"They could change light bulbs that us shorties can't reach," Buster offered.

"Was that you, Buster?"

"I can neither confirm nor deny your statement without my legal counsel present."

"Don't make me reach through the screen," Nathan threatened. "Well?"

"Their ambient temperature is insanely high. They can almost tolerate boiling water, and work effectively in that kind of heat—"

Nathan stopped her. "I'm kidding, Rivka. We can always use a good labor force with special abilities to tolerate environmental extremes. I'm not worried about that little detail. You helped us avert an interplanetary war. A war between two Federation signatories is the last thing we need. We already have a few of those, and they are ugly. We need to get in early and stop wars before they start, because once the shooting begins we have to wait until it's safe, and that means watching people die. I'm not a big fan of that."

"Neither am I, sir," Rivka agreed.

"Good job, Magistrate. New cases have been transmitted, and the High Chancellor has been informed. Go forth and be excellent to each other. Lowell out." The screen went blank.

"I wouldn't put those words into any more treaties," Grainger advised slowly.

"I won't, although it's not wrong." Rivka nodded wide-eyed for emphasis.

"And you call *me* strange!"

The End

You Have Been Judged - Judge, Jury, & Executioner, Book 1

If you like this book, please leave a review. This is a new series, so the only way I can decide whether to commit more time to it is by getting feedback from you, the readers. Your opinion matters to me. Continue or not? I have only so much time to craft new stories. Help me invest that time wisely. Plus, reviews buoy my spirits and stoke the fires of creativity.

Don't stop now! Keep turning the pages as Craig & Michael talk about their thoughts on this book and the overall project called the Age of Expansion.
Your new favorite legal eagle will return in Destroy the Corrupt.

Welcome to the Age of Expansion

AUTHOR INSIGHT - ORIGINAL OUTLINE

This is the original outline that I used as the basis to write this book. You'll see how my mind works and how much I have to fill in outside of the key points. Outline – I wrote this as if I was going to have a co-author, but decided that it was best for me to write the story. I love the premise, the characters, and the story. I had already written chapters one and two, so the outline starts with Chapter 3.

Enjoy!

Chapter 3 – meeting with High Chancellor Wyatt (introduce some of his back story here – see the character list at the end). He grills her regarding the murder. She admits to it all, even though she isn't sure what drove her to do what she does.

The High Chancellor is a vampire, but can't read minds. That is not that common. But he is old and has studied people his whole life. He can tell when people are lying.

She isn't. He can also sense the awakening nanocytes in her.

"You know the High Chancellor's Rangers have been disbanded?"

"Yes, but what does that have to do with anything?"

"They're not gone. We don't call them Rangers anymore. We call them Magistrates."

"You took Rangers and made them lawyers?"

"Meting out Justice is not for the faint of heart."

He leaves her to think about it without making an offer. She goes back to her cell confused. Is she going to be put to death for her crime or promoted? Keep in mind that she gets snippets of insight, but not from the vampire – his mind is far too disciplined to let errant thoughts leak out.

Chapter 4

Intergalactic guards whisk her away in the middle of the night. She is disoriented from lack of sleep but wakes up when they throw her on a two-person shuttle and fly her to space.

She arrives at a non-descript cargo transport. A prison ship. She's convinced that she's going to Jhiordaan. A well-built guy walks in to the interrogation room. He looks different, but he's wearing the barrister's jacket. He looks battle hardened. "Are you a Ranger?"

He puts his fingers to his lips. "We don't say that word anymore, barrister. I'm not a fan of ultimatums, but there are two possible outcomes here. One is completely in my control. The other is completely out of my control. If you want to keep your position as the Queen's Barrister, then join us, learn to handle yourself in a fight, including being able to use a wide variety of weapons. If you don't join us, then your fate is as a prisoner, something I have no influence over once you've entered that part of our legal system."

No choice but to join, but it's not that easy. There are tests. She has to interrogate three prisoners. One is innocent. The other two are guilty. She'll have to identify if any or all are innocent and serve Justice on the guilty, but only according to the crimes she can prove.

Chapter 5 (insert the legal mumbo jumbo to give it credibility)

Prisoner Number 1 – accused of capital theft (capital means that the death penalty attaches). Elements of the crime – intent to permanently deprive the owner of their property that is valued in excess of 10,000 credits. Must prove both intent (mens rea) and action (actus reus). This perp did it – stole an original piece of artwork, but the owner inflated the value of what was stolen (insurance fraud). So not capital theft, but misdemeanor theft. After figuring that out, she kicks the guy in the head and turns him loose. Justice is served.

Prisoner Number 2 – accused of assault and battery. He beat a man senseless. This guy is humble and contrite. He is ashamed and keeps admitting that he did it. She wonders why. Is he covering for someone, or did the victim drive him over the edge. She grills him on the fight. Turns out, the other guy threw the first punch, but the gentle man lost his shit in an adrenaline surge. He couldn't close the floodgates once they opened. She declares him innocent, but sends him to counselling so he doesn't fall into an uncontrolled rage. Had he killed the other man, nothing could have saved him.

Prisoner Number 3 – a Yollin, with carapace, mandibles, and two legs, which means he is of the lower class. He keeps calling her dickface. He is accused of murder. There's a video that shows he did it. He says he didn't. She thinks something is off. He says all Yollin look alike. She checks the records and they are as varied as humans. She gets into a shouting match and outmaneuvers him. He slips. "Guilty," she declares and then adds, "fuck you." He lunges and she kicks him so hard in the chest that it cracks his carapace. He falls back, spasms, and dies.

She is appalled. Again she has failed to control herself. The Magistrate enters the room clapping slowly.

"Welcome to the team."

Chapter 6

Training, lots of kick-ass training. Make it impressive. Include weapons of all type like, a chair, nunchakus, knives, pistols, a wine bottle, you name it – anything can be a weapon.

Keep in mind that everything a Magistrate does reflects on the legal system of the federation. Only the guilty can be punished. If punishment is directed, it must be carried out. A Magistrate can NEVER lose a fight to mete out Justice. If they don't think they can beat a perp, then they have to call for backup, which gives the perp a chance at trial and getting off.

Rivka becomes fanatical about training. She seeks to become uber-enhanced using the Pod-doc, but they don't let her go hog wild. "Work within yourself. We don't need

AUTHOR INSIGHT - ORIGINAL OUTLINE

any incredible hulks out there. A good Magistrate doesn't have to necessarily be the biggest and the baddest, she only needs to know when the advantage to deliver Justice is on her side."

Also, introduce sidekick Vered (see character details below). Vered absolutely doesn't get to mete out Justice. He is a bodyguard only. He will protect the Magistrate. If the Magistrate declares someone guilty and declares that Justice will be served, Vered must stay back, even if the Magistrate is getting her ass kicked and her life is in jeopardy. That is the federation legal code. Most Magistrates (the ones who weren't Rangers), will call for police and run the perp through the trial courts.

Chapter 7 (this might be two chapters worth of material)

Assigned a corvette (they are looking for a name for their ship throughout this book) to travel the galaxy on missions assigned by High Chancellor Wyatt. She gets to know the crew (see character list below). This corvette is outfitted with the miniaturized Etheric power supply and integrated gate technology that R2D2 developed with Ted's assistance.

They go to an outpost to adjudicate a case regarding criminal mischief, something that usually wouldn't get a barrister, because the local governor would handle it.

This case is unique in that the case is against the governor's daughter. Her name is Jayita, Jay for short. She is busting up stores on the space station. No one can control her. Finally the governor begged for an impartial party to deal with it. They sent the intern, but Wyatt knows the governor.

She'll be on display and reported on by these friends. She is tentative. The young girl is an ass, but Rivka suspects there's something deeper. Her sense kicks in and shows the abuse the girls has suffered at the hands of her mother whenever the father isn't around. He didn't believe her claims.

Magistrate puts the girl under her protection.

Rivka issues herself a search warrant and sneaks into the governor's quarters when she knows they aren't home. She finds evidence, but it is unclear who it points to, could implicate the governor. She makes the hard decision to leave the evidence behind. She schedules a private meeting with the governor, but lo and behold, the governor's spouse is there and won't let them talk.

Rivka clams up. She lets them do all the talking, and finally, Rivka declares her ruling. The girl is guilty of felony damage and making terroristic threats, she is condemned to life in prison. The parents are shocked and Rivka storms off.

She was lying. Her first case and she fails. She adds the girl to her crew and commits to putting her in the Pod-doc to change her appearance while Rivka second guesses her decision. She let her emotions guide her decision instead of the law. She should have confronted the family, but her only real evidence was inconclusive. Her telepathic flashes put her in conflict with what she could prove.

She calls her mentor (the former Ranger dude) and says she's not cut out to be a Magistrate. He apologizes to her. They knew what the situation was and resolving it was going to take a certain amount of heavy-handedness, while also recognizing that the governor was doing right by the

Federation. His successor probably would not. He applauded her solution, but cautioned her against doing it too often unless she wanted to pay for a bigger ship out of her pay.

"I can afford to buy a bigger ship?"

"That's just it. No you can't!" This dude (you pick a cool name for him that hasn't already been used in the Kurtherian universe) is the funniest guy he knows. Rivka doesn't always get his humor.

Chapter 9

More Pod-doc and more training as they return to home base (the non-descript cargo transport). She meets some other members of the group as they stop by to get their new assignments. This is an opportunity to detail what future story plots might look like.

- A serial killer on Planet X (start a listing of character and place names). Keep track as you go, or you'll be lost in a hurry, which means that I'll be lost

- A secret government facility that the brass thinks has been infiltrated, but they aren't sure. It could be an inside job, if they could only find if something was stolen.

- The Blood Trade. This was a thing in a number of books set on Earth (Second Dark Ages, Terry Henry Walton Chronicles, and Reclaiming Honor serieses). People are kidnapping the enhanced and draining their blood for non-enhanced to drink, boosts life and strength without getting the nanocytes programmed through a Pod-doc. This is on Yoll itself which is disconcerting. That's why they want a Magistrate to come in and deal with it.

AUTHOR INSIGHT - ORIGINAL OUTLINE

- A cozy murder on Planet Y, within the ruling circle. What was the reason why one of the ruling leadership's inner circle was murdered and who? They were on a retreat, only ten of them, but nine remain.

She gets to participate in the discussions and realizes how little they know without being there in person, seeing the scenes of the crimes and talking first-hand with the witnesses, otherwise, it's all hearsay, even witness statements because the questions could have been worded poorly. She starts to understand the Magistrate process better, which is akin to the judges of the old west who would show up to hear cases and then move on according to a schedule. The Magistrates here have that, too. Sometimes, they simply need to be somewhere and sit in judgment – the opportunity for a Judge Judy kind of scene should be in every book. The Magistrate hates sitting on a dais as two parties appear. Look at old Judge Judy scripts and see what is stupid funny. Then throw something like it in. The Magistrates can complain about their latest with the others whenever they get together for a beer. Maybe that's how each story can end with that trope as well. The Magistrates lamenting their latest cases (in a funny way "And then she grabs him by the balls and starts twisting! I wanted to rack her a good one upside the head, but that dude was a dick. I let it go until he was about to pass out before I stopped it. We both made our points. Justice is served, bitches..."

Chapter 10

Rivka's first assignment is to hear a trade dispute between neighboring systems Planet A and Planet B. The dispute has escalated to the point that the two systems are facing off, ready to fight a war. Rivka races into the middle of it and gets the parties back to the negotiating table, located on Planet B. She commits them to binding arbitration. She has the authority to determine how the contract details who is responsible for what.

They agree because they risk losing their Federation membership if they breach the contract. They go back and forth, each side (they are aliens, make them cool) tries to get Rivka alone to see how their position should dominate. She can't interpret the flashes she gets from their minds, so she doesn't know who to believe.

Both sides are pushy and she ends the side conversations with fist fights as they try to physically intimidate her. She beats the crap out of both sides (their lackeys, the prime negotiators would never dirty their hands with the wet work, unlike the Magistrates).

She returns to the corvette to think.

Chapter 11

As she determines a contract that screws each negotiator but is in the best interest of both their people, there's a big argument. She hits the table so hard, it breaks in half. She hands the trade deal contract to each party to sign. They both point to the broken table. "Just sign it on your laps, for fuck's sake!"

At that point, a bomb goes off. Rivka's nanos save her life, but one of the main negotiators (Planet A) is dead and the other is barely injured. Even in her pain-fogged stupor, she sees that they may have crossed the line to war as the one side will accuse the other of setting off the bomb.

AUTHOR INSIGHT - ORIGINAL OUTLINE

She determines two courses of action. Get both parties to sign the contract to avert the war, and then find who planted the bomb.

The rest of this chapter is medical recovery and posturing. Everything is spinning out of control.

Chapter 12

Rivka brings her team to Planet B and starts the investigation. She suspects it was someone local as they had the access. The aliens from Planet A were restricted in their movements, ostensibly for their own safety.

Planet A's propaganda war was turning the A population against B. Rivka starts at the scene of the bombing. She feels like it should affect her, but doesn't. She is looking at the scene dispassionately. There's a blood stain in one area. The blood was hers. Now, it's evidence in a crime.

I'm a Magistrate. I will solve this crime and bring the motherfuckers responsible to Justice. I know there's more than one. Wherever it leads, I'll follow. If I have to fuck people up along the way, so be it.

Throw out some bombing clues – parts of a detonator, residue, location, access to the scene beforehand, timing of the explosion suggests remote detonation, but who knew when the contract would be signed and at that moment?

Chapter 13

Rivka takes evidence samples back to the corvette to study them, leaving her team on the planet. Red is out of his element because there are no humans that he can impress with his looks. Jay and Red explore the area but

AUTHOR INSIGHT - ORIGINAL OUTLINE

stand out. They can go nowhere without the feeling of being watched.

"Fuck it. Sounds like we need the direct approach." They go from store to store and ask the same question. "Why do you hate Planet B?"

The response is canned, almost scripted. That's when they figure the propaganda machine on Planet A is running at full speed. They head for the media center and find that it's a planet wide broadcast and run entirely by the government. They haven't had free elections.

Ever.

Because the people always thought they had a choice, but they never did. They were told what to believe. No matter which candidate won the election, the people would always get more of the same.

Red and Jay report this to Rivka. She is not surprised. Her analysis is complete. It's inconclusive. The perps were good enough that the explosives were commonly used on both planets. Nothing indicates one side over the other.

Rivka enjoyed their tale of the direct action approach. "I'm on my way. We'll see if the Magistrate can get some straight answers." She's now starting to feel her role and willing to use some of the authority of her position. She wants to talk with Planet A's leader, alone.

Chapter 14

Rivka is granted an audience, but not alone. The leader can't shield his thoughts and is worried that Planet A will be found out. He's a lackey, but complicit. The shadow government runs everything. Rivka's insight shows her faceless entities behind the throne, as it may be.

But she brushes that off as it seems to lead her away from her mission. Her job is to find and punish the bomber and get the trade agreement signed. There's overlap between the bombing and the shadow government, of course, but she has to find the bomber as she knows that she'll get nowhere coming at the problem from the top down. People at the bottom were much more likely to talk.

She also wanted to explore the limits of her leverage. Could she hold her emotions at bay while people lied to her? It was a game of mental chess. Was she prepared to play?

She strong-arms the building security to get a complete list of all people who were in the building for a full day prior. Rivka puts the EI (Cosmo) on finding all the video from within the building and compiling a full portfolio.

Rivka matches all the names and pictures with people in the videos and she finds a few that aren't accounted for. The Planet B building security wonder how that could happen and have no helpful ideas. Rivka is stymied, until Jay shows her an alternate way into the building.

And there's a camera, but the video feed doesn't go to security. Planet B security help her tap it and trace it. She holds off the government leaders, slapping them in the head with their Federation charter which clearly delineates that Magistrates will be given full support when investigating crimes that they were called to.

"But we didn't call you to investigate the bombing," they argue.

"But you called me to negotiate the trade pact. Causation is insufficient in establishing that a crime has been committed, but Rivka declares that the two are causally related, ergo, she was called, now get the fuck out of my way.

Chapter 15

They find where the feed terminates, an old building with a revolving door of renters. They will never find the video, but they do find who rented the space where the fiber ends. They track that alien down. He is terrified as he's running for his life.

Why?

Because I'm a loose end. They don't like loose ends. Rivka sees a face in a flash from the alien's mind. One of the members of the Planet B party.

Let the hands-on interrogation begin. Bring Yutta to me!

Oh hell, no. He runs. The team chases him through the alien city and into the countryside. Before they can catch him, he jumps off a cliff to his death.

Son of a bitch.

Chapter 16

Back to the scene of the crime. "What are we missing?"

"Evidence?" Red suggests.

"No shit. Why would we have no evidence? How in the hell can someone waltz in here and plant a bomb, even if they did use the back door? I want the entire negotiating party back here, from both sides."

"Planet A people went home."

"I don't give a shit. Bring them back! Who doesn't understand the definition of 'binding arbitration?' Get them back here. We have a contract to sign."

She expects that the perps will try again. She turns Jay and Red loose to cover the back door. She'll check everyone who joins her in the new meeting room.

Bringing the parties together will neither be quick nor easy. She is constantly vigilant, looking for the minions of the shadow government. She stays in the room they'll use, denying access to everyone.

She sees the lurkers, at the edge of vision, always, peeking around corners and watching. She gives them the finger.

Chapter 17

Racing toward the signing. Planet B's negotiator (Miento) wants to go back to the drawing board. Rivka smiles and shakes her head.

"The agreement was finished. We're not going to let an ass-hugging terrorist to walk us backward. Once you two sign, then the reason for the terrorism will no longer exist. This contract will be iron clad. The one to violate it will be blockaded by Federation ships. Your planet will wither and die. If there are some anarchists who want them, then it's incumbent upon you to find them. That will be an internal issue, so sign the fucking contract as the arbitrator has determined."

Miento tries to stall.

"Why are you stalling? Your murderous thugs are late? I know it was your merry band who conducted the bombing. I know why the good people of Planet A put up with your bullshit. You have stuff they need and they have stuff you need. Your delays are complete and utter bullshit. In lawyerese, if you refuse to sign a properly negotiated contract, it'll go into effect and will be binding in any case."

"But then my name won't be on it," the alien sighs. He puts down the pen and walks away.

"Binding!" Rivka yells after him.

Meanwhile Red and Jay intercept the assassination team, but they're good. Red is able to off a couple, but the other four drive them back. Jay is looking for cover. She doesn't mind breaking into places, but when the lead starts flying, she's running for cover.

Planet A signs and Rivka signs as the formal arbiter. She indicates that Planet B is a willing party and attaches the signed arbitration document as proof of validity in lieu of signature.

She transmits the document to the corvette for further transmission to the Federation.

But the corvette is getting jammed.

"Too late boys," when Red and Jay run into the room with the four assassins hot on their tail. "Contract is a sealed deal."

They start firing and the Planet A delegation and Rivka's team are trapped in the room. She didn't bring a pistol. She only had knives and what was in the room. Red hands his weapon to her.

"A crime to stop a valid negotiation on top of another crime to cover up the first crime."

"They don't look like they're trying to cover anything, which means they are guilty."

Rivka dumps the conference table on its side and they wait. The men burst into the room. She empties the pistol. They are wearing body armor, but so is she. She is able to find a couple soft points, but runs out of ammo before she runs out of targets. She downs the third with a thrown knife, but the fourth knocks Red out.

Rivka takes him on – epic fight, Rivka improvises a weapon and delivers the killing blow. She kicks his corpse as her chest heaves with each breath. "Justice is served, jiz ball."

Chapter 18

The corvette is still being jammed. Planet A's fleet comes to the rescue after being summoned by a local broadcast that broke through the jamming signal. The Planet A forces surround the corvette and break the jam.

The contract is transmitted.

"It's over," Rivka declares.

"Is it?" Red asks. She recovers her knives, hands his pistol back, and together they hurry out to meet with the government leader.

"But it's not signed..." he stutters.

"But it is," she said, pointing to his signature on the binding arbitration agreement. "It's like you signed it. Good luck telling your masters that you committed them to this."

"Wait! You can't leave me here. I request asylum!"

Rivka looks at the man. "Fuck off." And walks away. He throws himself at her feet. "No, really. Fuck off. You can either figure out how to make this work, or you can all kill each other. At this point? It's not my problem. I'm sorry. I think you might not have heard." She grabs his face in both her hands. "FUCK. OFF."

AUTHOR INSIGHT - ORIGINAL OUTLINE

He is in the fetal position and crying when they leave and go back to the corvette.

After they return to their ship, they allow a delegation from Planet B on board.

The conversation is about what Planet B can do to make sure the agreement is implemented without causing more grief from Planet A. She senses regime change is coming.

Especially since Cosmo tapped the media broadcast. They start sending out messages about how friendly B is and that the contract would usher in a new era of prosperity for all of A's people.

Chapter 19

Rivka declares victory, her role complete and heads back to home base.

Her debrief with her mentor is less than stellar. His point was that she should have controlled the situation better from the beginning. Allowing a bomb into the location where they were working was unacceptable.

From the top of the mountain to the deepest valley she falls. "But I got the law right, didn't I?"

"Sure, but any goofy fucker can get that part right. It's how you massage it into place without beating people over the head with it that will make you great."

"Then why do I train so hard to beat people over the head?"

"Because we're not perfect. We're Magistrates. Let me buy you a beer so we can tell lies in the peace and comfort of our own drunken stupor."

Planet A - Pretaria. Known for its hotter-than-average,

arid climate. Planet A's people - Pretarians. Average between 7' - 9' tall, wear their hair long with small-diameter braids on each side of their face (one per side). Anyone seen with shorn hair is outcaste or has been judged a criminal. Orange skin tones, yellow eyes with kidney-shaped pupils (think goat), leathery skin from sun exposure, and a penchant for wearing lots of clacking beads.

Planet A names - Maseer, Rhonali, Tinashi, Ngobo, Sinraloo

Planet B - Keome, desert-ish - think red rocks of Colorado color with deep peatish colored lakes. Flat surface with craters (canyon-y) Planet B's people - Tall, 7 or 8 feet, kind of chameleonable (like all the very very descriptive adjectives - able, ish, y. LOL). bi-pedal, long, long, multi-armed with eyes all around that move like an owl.

Miento (primary), Yus (secondary), Suarpok (priest), Ome (heroine), Yutta (bad guy)

THE PLAYERS

Rivka Anoa (Main Character)—Age 25. Lean and athletic build. Blonde hair with golden-blue hazel eyes. Found walking down an alley on the QBBS *Meredith Reynolds* as a two-year-old, covered in someone else's blood. Parents never found. Taken in and raised by older couple. Graduated ELA at age 20. Commissioned as a tribunal officer at age 22. Worked in the general Federation legal office as a trial advocate for one year and an intern for the last two. She caught the eye of Bethany Anne at some point and was labeled the Queen's Barrister. Finally passes her exams and is a full barrister. Plays ukulele but tries to hide it.

Vered "Red" (Sidekick) – "Muscle" assigned to protect Rivka. V shape. Caramel skin with jet black hair and brown eyes. Melting pot of ethnic influence – exotic beauty in a seductive man-candy package, all hiding a bad-ass warrior underneath. Hates dogs and cats and lets that color his opinion of Weres. There is no sexual tension between Red and Rivka. But he is more than happy to hit on women wherever they go, but not to the detriment of doing his job as a bodyguard.

Grainger – Former Ranger turned Magistrate. Tall and well-built. Hardcore combat veteran. His real name is Lieblen Schlongheim.

Chaz – EI assigned to Rivka and residing in the newly-commissioned corvette carrying Rivka and her unit.

Hamlet – The cat. Comic relief and occasional trouble-maker throughout the series.

Jayita – The vagrant daughter of the governor, who turned out to have been abused (not sexually, but emotionally and physically beaten) by the governor's wife. She is dainty, five foot and less than a hundred pounds (but we use metric in space, so whatever that is). She is lean and dexterous like a thief, but that's only because she always felt she was on the run. They will eventually put her into the Pod-doc to change her appearance, but it doesn't do much. She has the same body. Her face becomes a little more round, her hair long and brown (or pink or blonde), and her eyes are now so dark brown that her pupils can no longer be distinguished. It gives her a bit of a creepy look that she uses on occasion to intimidate people (she stares without blinking).

Atticus "Custer" Tikabow – Rivka's foil and later love interest. Attended Earth Etheric Academy with Rivka and Rivka's friend, who disappeared mysteriously. Custer was the main suspect in the disappearance, but no evidence was ever found to prove his involvement. Sandy hair with green eyes, tall and muscular without being bulky. Always wears a sneaky smile and prefers representing the accused. Most people see him as a sleazy defense lawyer.

High Chancellor Wyatt – A heavily Pod-doc enhanced humanoid with vampire capabilities (glowing red eyes and fangs) Head of the Federation Justice System. Turned to vampire by BA to help him be the face of the law (vampires get fewer arguments from people). Was a lawyer for Yoll before BA became the Queen. Practiced as a lawyer throughout the Empire's colonies for a few decades as a non-Yollin. Close follower and employee of BA, but not high-profile. Good lawyers aren't in the spotlight. BA develops a grudging trust of Wyatt and sets him up with Lance Reynolds. Lance needs someone who can make the legal wheels turn to bring the Federation into a reality. Wyatt is that kind of lawyer—jaded, cynical, practical, and ruthless when he needs to be.)

AUTHOR NOTES - CRAIG MARTELLE

WRITTEN JUNE 18, 2018

You are still reading! Thank you so much. It doesn't get much better than that.

I went to the dentist, and they asked what I do. A sci-fi author with lots of titles. See my books in Barnes & Noble, too. Dr. Tyler Ingersoll in Fairbanks did a bang-up job on a filling that had gone astray, so I asked him if he'd like me to put one of his characters in a book. So here he is, Dr. Tyler Toofakre, the dentist who works on our favorite barrister. The persona that my dentist wanted was complete normalcy. Most dentists on TV are portrayed as weird or creepy. It's hard not to notice. In cozy mysteries, if there's a dentist? Keep your eye on that guy... As far as

Toofakre? I think I'll make him a recurring character. When the universe gets to be too much, sometimes it's nice to live vicariously through those with more staid lives.

Ingersoll Family Dentistry, Fairbanks, Alaska. Nothing like gaining new fans. The Fairbanks community as a whole is supportive.

I've gone with Ricciardo Domesta (do me, sta) by Rocco Lauria for the bureaucrat, only named a couple times.

But I found that I needed an AI who would help out during interrogations and do criminal law research. Lexis/Nexis is the legal database lawyers use, so the AI will be Lexi Malachi, with props to Melissa Giese for Malachi. I'll also at some point use Felcario Renaldo Squitieri, suggested by Melissa Williams, with more props. Thank you guys for your quick, broad-ranging, and far-reaching suggestions. I know that I can always count on you (yinz in Pittsburghese).

Shout out to Karen Cabael for offering Chaz Woodworth the Third, although Karen may have expected this name to be used for a minor antagonist, I have a soft spot for the name Charles. Charles Martel was the grandfather of Charles the Great, known by his Romanized name, Charlemagne, from whom I'm descended on my father's side. My paternal grandfather was named Charles. My mother's dad was also named Charles, but he went by Chaz. I think we'll use this for the EI on board Rivka's ship —Chaz Woodworth the Third, an EI I hope you grow to love:)

And then there are the more in-depth names for the planetary squabble. More people stepped up with intensity in ten cities! Tracey Byrnes and Jael Sheppard. I also named one of the Magistrates after Jael.

Tracey Byrnes Planet A—Pretaria. Known for its hotter-than-average arid climate. Planet A's people—Pretarians. Average between 7' - 9' tall, wear their hair long with small-diameter braids on each side of their face (one per side). Anyone seen with shorn hair is outcast or has been judged a criminal. Orange skin tones, yellow eyes with kidney-shaped pupils (think goat), leathery skin from sun exposure, and a penchant for wearing lots of clacking beads. Planet A names —Maseer, Rhonali, Tinashi, Ngobo, Sinraloo.

Jael Sheppard New Planet B—Keome, desert-ish, think red rocks of Colorado color with deep peatish-colored lakes. Flat surface with craters (canyon-y). Planet A's people—Tall, 7 or 8 feet, kind of chameleonable (like all the very descriptive adjectives—able, ish, y. LOL). Bi-pedal, long, long, multi-armed with eyes all around. They could move like an owl. (the eyes, I mean, although... winged would kind of be cool). Yus (primary), Miento (secondary), Suarpok (priest), Ome (heroine), Yutta (bad guy)

And then there's me and home. I'll be here for three months straight without traveling. I'm excited about that. I need to rest and recover and tell some more and varied stories before the fall travel starts. Temps are sweet here at home. Mosquitoes are horrendous, but it's cool enough to keep 100% of my body covered, including a mosquito head net. It's good that there are no people about. That's not a look I want to be known for.

I hope everyone enjoyed this story. It was fun to write in a way that I found most relaxing.

AUTHOR NOTES - CRAIG MARTELLE

Peace, fellow humans.

* * *

Please join my Newsletter (www.craigmartelle.com – please, please, please sign up!), or you can follow me on Facebook since you'll get the same opportunity to pick up the books for only 99 cents on that first day they are published.

If you liked this story, you might like some of my other books. You can join my mailing list by dropping by my website **www.craigmartelle.com** or if you have any comments, shoot me a note at craig@craigmartelle.com. I am always happy to hear from people who've read my work. I try to answer every email I receive.

If you liked the story, please write a short review for me on Amazon. I greatly appreciate any kind words, even one or two sentences go a long way. The number of reviews an ebook receives greatly improves how well an ebook does on Amazon.

Amazon - www.amazon.com/author/craigmartelle
BookBub - https://www.bookbub.com/authors/craig-martelle
Facebook - www.facebook.com/authorcraigmartelle
My web page - www.craigmartelle.com

That's it—break's over, back to writing the next book. Peace, fellow humans.

AUTHOR NOTES - MICHAEL ANDERLE

JUNE 20, 2018

THANK YOU for making it all the way through Rivka's story, to these *Author Notes* in the back.

When the story came together for Rivka, I have to admit I was pretty excited. I'm a 'minor Judge Dredd fan. (No, seriously, kinda minor.)

I've seen both movies (the Karl Urban is better) and read a few of the comics, which means probably three.

However, Justice is something that speaks to me. When you meld it with action and attitude, it is like sweet nectar to a bee, and I want to read it. Now, Craig did Rivka a bit differently than I expected, and he modified the origination of the group in a way I did not see coming.

The Queen's Rangers were disbanded (I should know this, I made it happen), but my characters are predominately in another section of the universe busy NOT being Rangers. Craig, on the other hand, took the Rangers and amped them up.

I'm rather jealous of that idea, personally.

Craig is a lawyer (please don't hold that against him), and he brings this knowledge into the series. When he gave me the little bit from the bar scene in the very beginning—when she beats the crap out of the guy but gives him the law as she does it—I was *enthralled*.

And I said, "Please sir, can I have some more?"

Craig would drop little pieces to me from time and time, reeling me in like the little literary drug dealer he is. Finally, I just told him to give it all to me as soon as he could. I didn't have the time nor inclination to be spoon-fed anymore.

So I read it. Stayed up late, in fact. Damn near knocked the shit out of my nose by using my iPad and falling asleep. Just catching the iPad before it pancaked my schnoz woke me up in a horribly painful fashion.

Now *you* have read the story, and I hope that you, like me, are on the Rivka bandwagon. Shaking our fists at the bad guys *(or girls...or aliens...)* and yelling, "Kick their asses, Rivka!"

Until the next story, I'm biding my time...impatiently...and telling Craig, "Hurry your ass up! I have a need for more Rivka!"

Ad Aeternitatem.

Michael

BOOKS BY CRAIG MARTELLE

Craig Martelle's other books (listed by series)

Terry Henry Walton Chronicles (co-written with Michael Anderle) – a post-apocalyptic paranormal adventure

Gateway to the Universe (co-written with Justin Sloan & Michael Anderle) – this book transitions the characters from the Terry Henry Walton Chronicles to The Bad Company

The Bad Company (co-written with Michael Anderle) – a military science fiction space opera

End Times Alaska (also available in audio) – a Permuted Press publication – a post-apocalyptic survivalist adventure

The Free Trader – a Young Adult Science Fiction Action Adventure

Cygnus Space Opera – A Young Adult Space Opera (set in the Free Trader universe)

Darklanding (co-written with Scott Moon) – a Space Western

Rick Banik – Spy & Terrorism Action Adventure

Become a Successful Indie Author – a non-fiction work

BOOKS BY MICHAEL ANDERLE

For a complete list of books by Michael Anderle, please visit:

www.lmbpn.com/ma-books/

All LMBPN Audiobooks are Available at Audible.com and iTunes

To see all LMBPN audiobooks, including those written by Michael Anderle please visit:

www.lmbpn.com/audible

CONNECT WITH THE AUTHORS

Craig Martelle Social

Website & Newsletter:
http://www.craigmartelle.com

Facebook:
https://www.facebook.com/AuthorCraigMartelle/

Michael Anderle Social

Website: http://kurtherianbooks.com/

Email List: http://kurtherianbooks.com/email-list/
Facebook:
https://www.facebook.com/TheKurtherianGambitBooks/

Made in the USA
Middletown, DE
30 August 2018